S0-AZD-733

3 4028 07786 5302
HARRIS COUNTY PUBLIC LIBRARY

J Sander
Sanders, Stephanie
Villain School : good
curses evil

$6.99
ocn701481341
1st U.S. ed.   11/14/2011

WITHDRAWN

VILI

GOO

VILLAIN SCHOOL
Good Curses Evil

Stephanie S. Sanders

BLOOMSBURY

NEW YORK BERLIN LONDON SYDNEY

Copyright © 2011 by Stephanie S. Sanders
Bat illustrations © 2011 by Esy Casey
All rights reserved. No part of this book may be reproduced or transmitted in any form
or by any means, electronic or mechanical, including photocopying, recording, or by any
information storage and retrieval system, without permission in writing from the publisher.

First published in the United States of America in August 2011
by Bloomsbury Books for Young Readers
www.bloomsburykids.com

For information about permission to reproduce selections from this book, write to
Permissions, Bloomsbury BFYR, 175 Fifth Avenue, New York, New York 10010

Library of Congress Cataloging-in-Publication Data
Sanders, Stephanie (Stephanie Summer).
Villain School : good curses evil / Stephanie Sanders.—1st U.S. ed.
p.   cm.
Summary: Twelve-year-old Rune Drexler is struggling in his classes
at Master Dreadthorn's School for Wayward Villains and will be exiled unless
he and his friends, Countess Jezebel Dracula and Big Bad Wolf Junior,
can succeed at a nearly impossible Plot.
ISBN 978-1-59990-610-2 (hardback) • ISBN 978-1-59990-848-9 (paperback)
[1. Adventure and adventurers—Fiction. 2. Magic—Fiction. 3. Schools—Fiction.
4. Best friends—Fiction. 5. Friendship—Fiction. 6. Good and evil—Fiction.] I. Title.
PZ7.S1978832Vil 2011   [Fic]—dc22   2010050180

Book design by Donna Mark
Typeset by Westchester Book Composition
Printed in the U.S.A. by Quad/Graphics, Fairfield, Pennsylvania
2 4 6 8 10 9 7 5 3 1 (hardback)
2 4 6 8 10 9 7 5 3 1 (paperback)

All papers used by Bloomsbury Publishing, Inc., are natural, recyclable products
made from wood grown in well-managed forests. The manufacturing processes
conform to the environmental regulations of the country of origin.

For Ben, Kyra, and Kaelyn. You know why.

Contents

VILLAIN SCHOOL
Good Curses Evil

CHAPTER ONE

Detention

Remember, even the best death ray is no guarantee of success . . ."

My raven quill quivered furiously as I doodled on my parchment, pretending to take notes. At the front of the dungeon room, Master Dreadthorn droned on and on *and on*. The Master's lecture on the history of villainy had ceased to be interesting nearly an hour ago when he'd finished talking about supervillains and moved on to evil theory.

"You'll notice this is explained in the chart on page one thousand nine hundred seventy-eight of *Centuries of Villainy* . . ."

Blah. Blah. Blah. His voice began to sound like a balloon that had been filled with air and squeezed at the end so that the air leaks out slowly, morphing the

Master's voice into a long series of whiny squeaks that never seemed to end.

Oblivious, I continued doodling a series of cartoon boxes. In the first one, goblins came upon an unsuspecting cat. In the second box, the goblins attacked, taking the cat by surprise. In the third, the cat sprouted bat wings and fangs. I was just finishing up the final cartoon in which the cat was extraordinarily fat and licking his lips with a forked tongue, the ground around him littered with a few detached goblin body parts, when I noticed the room was strangely quiet.

"Interesting notes, Rune," a smooth, menacing voice said from just behind my left ear. I turned slowly to find the Dread Master staring at me. Busted.

"Uh ... um ... ," I stammered stupidly.

"What is white when it's dirty and black when it is clean?" the Master asked.

"Uh ... um ... ," I stammered stupidly some more. Master Dreadthorn liked to torture students—especially screwups like me—with riddles that were impossible to answer.

"Your hair?" I said, smiling up at the Dread Master. He didn't return the favor. I quickly explained. "You know, because dandruff is white and would make hair dirty."

Master Dreadthorn bored into me with his ink-black

eyes. I tried desperately to save myself. "But not your hair. I don't mean your hair because obviously you don't have dandruff, and your hair's not dirty, and that's not the right answer, is it?"

"The answer is a blackboard," he said. "Detention, Rune. Midnight. In my study."

Any ordinary kid at any ordinary school would've gotten off with just a warning. I mean, I tried to answer his ridiculous riddle, right? But this was no ordinary school.

This was Master Dreadthorn's School for Wayward Villains. It's like military school for children whose parents were evil. Bad guys. *Villains.* And how does a child end up in evil villain military school? Simple. By trying to be good.

Except me. I mean, I hadn't exactly done something good. I was placed in the school because of my family. I never knew my mom, but my dad is a warlock. A very powerful warlock, sure, but nobody a non-villain would've heard of. Nobody the Grimm Brothers would have written home about. His name is Veldin Drexler. But everyone here just calls him Master Dreadthorn.

* * *

"You are so dead," a voice said next to me as I shuffled down the murky cave tunnel with my books. It was

Wolf Junior. The torches that lined the wall were extra-acrid today, making my eyes sting.

"Rune, are you crying?" another voice asked from beside me.

It was Countess Jezebel, Dracula's daughter. She was here because once she told her dad that hot cocoa tasted better than blood. He might have overlooked that little incident if he hadn't found her supersecret stash of chocolate the next day. Turned out Jez had never really taken to the vampire diet; she'd been switching out her blood for other food—mostly of the cocoa variety—for years. Count Dracula has a very important image to maintain. A vampire daughter who didn't like blood? It was extremely embarrassing.

"No, Jezebel. I am *not* crying," I answered.

"Looks like tears to me," Wolf said.

Jezebel and I looked pretty much like normal humans (except for her fangs and ultrawhite skin). But Wolf Junior, on the other hand . . . he looked just like his dad—Big Bad Wolf Senior. Only, Junior walked around on two legs instead of four. His pink doggy tongue lolled stupidly from his snout as he panted in anticipation of my anger.

"Just plug it, Wolf," I said. "I'm not in the mood."

Wolf Junior was here because when he was six, he saved a human child from drowning. Then his dad found out. It wasn't pretty. He huffed and puffed and shipped Wolf off to this place.

"And suck that ugly thing back into your mouth. Your breath smells like a fart swamp," I said.

Wolf stuck his tongue out even farther at me, muttered something that might have been "*Touchy*," and shuffled ahead to join the rest of his pack of brown-nosers. And they really had brown noses ... or black ones or beaks. They were the half-breeds, or halfsies— children of animal villains who'd taken on human forms long enough to produce kids. Halfsies were the result.

Technically, Jezebel and I were halfsies too: villain fathers, human mothers. Real, full-blood villains were rare—probably because two full-grown villains were more likely to kill each other than get married and have kids. Neither Jez nor I ever got to know our moms.

"His hair, Rune? The answer was so obvious. Chalk is white. It makes a blackboard dirty," Jezebel said.

I just glared at her.

"Whaddaya think he's going to do to you?" Jezebel asked me.

"Who?" I asked. But I knew what she meant.

"Your dad."

"I'll find out at midnight, won't I?"

"It'll probably be scrubbing slug slime off the floors. Or maybe gathering dragon fire for the torches. Or it might be—"

"Cat-a-bats, Jez! Don't you have some chocolate cookies to bake or something?"

She huffed, turned up her nose, and stormed down the hallway. The truth is, Jezebel was right—these were all valid possibilities. Detention was usually a painful or demeaning task. No chalkboard erasers for me. No writing "I will not doodle in History of Villainy class" a hundred times on the blackboard. And I'd screwed up a lot lately too. I had a funny feeling that this time the punishment would be severe.

I slinked back to my dormitory, where my roommate, Chad, was reading *Spells for Dummies.*

What? A villain can't be named Chad?

"Hey, Rune," he said. "Want to try my latest batch of cookies?"

Chad was the son of the witch who tried to eat Hansel and Gretel. She wasn't really much of a mom, either. She'd pretty much shipped him off to school and never talked to him again, except for the occasional letter.

Chad wasn't too good at most spells, but he was a great cook. We always had plenty of gingerbread men on hand with gumdrop buttons and everything. Only, Chad always had to break their heads off with his toy guillotine so the other kids wouldn't make fun of him.

"You heard?" I asked.

Chad looked up shyly from his book, his puppy-dog eyes framed with thick, ridiculous glasses. A fresh tray of cookies greeted me from my bedside table.

"Heard what?" Chad asked. He was trying to play dumb, but I wasn't fooled. Not only was Chad bad at spells, he was also a bad liar. Not a good sign for a villain-in-training. Not good at all.

"You wouldn't have baked me cookies unless you'd heard," I said. Of course, that wasn't really true. Chad would've baked cookies just for the fun of it.

"I heard. Whaddaya think it'll be? Scrubbing slug slime?" he asked, closing his book and hopping down from the top bunk of his bed.

The bottom bunk was vacant. We used to be three, but Ivan—a huge kid who was rumored to be the son of a giant—didn't qualify as a villain. He lost his place at the school after the first month. Turned out his dad really wasn't the giant from the top of the beanstalk. He was actually just some jolly green guy who talked human kids into eating their vegetables. Kind of embarrassing for Ivan.

"Slug slime is getting a lot of votes tonight," I said.

I threw down my books on the bed and picked up a gingerbread man, chomping off his left arm. I noticed Chad hadn't chopped off this batch's heads yet, and when I bit the tiny cookie's arm off, I could see why.

The little man's frosting mouth turned from a smile to an O of alarm as he shrieked in agony.

"My arm! Oh, my *poor arm*!"

I nearly dropped the cookie in surprise. "That's new," I said, raising one eyebrow at Chad.

"Yep. I bewitched the cookies to scream when you bite them. The ones with blue gumdrops ooze red frosting when you bite off their heads. I discovered I'm not too bad with spells if I use them in conjunction with baking."

"*Nice*," I said, munching appreciatively until the muffled screams of the cookie were silent.

Love of baking and lack of lying capabilities weren't Chad's only unvillain-ish attributes. He also didn't look the part. Take me, for instance. Sure, I had the black hair and pale, waxy complexion (with a few zits now and then), not to mention my dad's black eyes. But I also *dressed* the part. I wore the swirling black velvet cloak, the black leather boots, the high-collared button-up shirts. Okay, I tripped on the cloak sometimes, the boots gave me blisters, and the shirts gagged my throat, but it was an *image*.

Chad, on the other hand . . . Let's just say if someone met him in a dark alley, they wouldn't exactly cringe in fear. Their neck hairs probably wouldn't even prickle. In fact, once the blond, curly-haired, blue-eyed, freckle-faced, bespectacled form of Chad emerged with a tray of freshly baked gingerbread cookies, most people would want to adopt him.

"Take some to the Dread Master. Maybe it'll soften him up," Chad suggested.

"Anything's worth a try," I said.

Midnight (otherwise known as the hour of my impending doom) wasn't that far away, actually. All the classes at Master Dreadthorn's School for Wayward Villains were held at night, underground. Mostly it was because half the student body couldn't endure sunshine. We got a lot of vampires and troll halfsies. Sure, they didn't erupt into flames or turn to complete stone in the sun. They were just halfsies after all. But the vamps would get nasty rashes, and the trolls would turn *partially* to stone—usually their legs or just one arm or something. Which reminded me . . .

"Hey, Chad, did you hear about Orksy Toren?"

"No, what'd he do this time?"

"Well, that girl from Mad Science class—you know the one? With snakes on her head? Anyway, she dared him to go outside. In the sun."

"He didn't do it!" Chad said.

"Oh, he did. It was hilarious! Orksy ended up turning his butt into stone for three hours. He just fell over on his rump and had to be dragged to the nurse."

"Trolls are so dumb," Chad said, rolling his eyes—which looked really weird because his glasses magnified his eyes so they looked huge. He turned his gaze toward my desk. "Oh, Newt's looking kinda ashy. I think he's hungry."

I lifted the lid to a glass tank and pulled out Eye of Newt, my pet salamander. When I was just a kid, I'd jinxed him in Spelling class (spell-casting, that is—nothing so normal as learning to spell *c-a-t*). I accidentally turned Newt into a Cyclops. Master Stiltskin, the Spelling instructor, let me keep him.

"For practice," he had said. Out of all the Villain Masters at the school, Master Stiltskin was the least villain-ish. He was a really old warlock with a hunched back and long, white hair and an equally long, white beard. Rumpelstiltskin had been his granddad. The guy who could spin straw into gold? But now Master Stiltskin was retired from villaining. He just taught Spelling as a hobby.

"Hey, Newt," I said, stroking the salamander's slimy back. He turned his one eye up at me and blinked. Or winked. "Ya hungry?"

Eye of Newt flicked out his tongue at me; his black body smoldered red. I set him back in his glass tank, pulled out a container of fire ants, and dumped them into Newt's cage. Quick as lightning, his tongue flicked out like a flame and licked up all the ants. Happy and full, his back caught on fire.

"Now, quit that, Newt. You'll singe your wood-chips," I said before turning back to Chad.

"I heard there's a field trip to Mistress Morgana's next full moon," Chad said.

"What! No! Are you kidding me? We have to endure those snobs again?" I said.

Once a month, during full moon, classes were halted so the werewolves could rant and rave while the rest of us went on field trips. I'm not talking zoos and muse-ums. Villain field trips meant visiting graveyards or caves or sometimes even stealing artifacts or magical items from wealthy, important humans. The next full moon was just a few days away.

Mistress Morgana's School for Exemplary Villains was the hated rival of our own school. Morgana's was for all the snooty, boot-licking villain kids who were never good a day in their evil lives.

"That means a trip down the coast," Chad was kind enough to point out—I get a little seasick.

"Great, I get to barf all the way."

Morgana's school was located in an extravagant castle perched on a cliff overlooking the sea. Talk about *posh*. They had it so cushy there.

Mistress Morgana was a sinister beauty who'd been

turning black hearts crustier since the days of King Arthur. She and her band of wicked high-and-mighties were always rubbing our noses in the fact that we all had (at least once in our lives) been good and, therefore, less than perfect.

"Yep. Since it's harvest moon, there's going to be a Plot," Chad said. I thought I saw him quivering just a bit.

"No way!" I said.

A Plot was like the equivalent of a sporting event or dance for villains. Kids were usually selected by lottery to participate. It typically involved something evil and dangerous to be carried out on unsuspecting humans. Most people have heard about thefts of famous paintings or an illness like chicken pox making a whole town sick at once. Those were the result of villain school Plots. The extinction of the unicorn? A Plot. Mount Vesuvius? Another Plot. The myth that green, leafy vegetables are good for kids? That was one of the worst Plots ever.

I didn't have much time to think about Plots or the field trip to Mistress Morgana's because at that moment, the Great Clock—a huge, monstrous thing with scaly and clawed creatures frozen in hideous, leering poses all around it—struck the hour. Midnight. I was late.

CHAPTER TWO

A Plot

Rune, Rune, Rune," the Dread Master said.

I stood at the door to his study, waiting for the old man to invite me in. That wasn't really fair. I mean, he was *my* old man, but he wasn't all that old. Warlocks don't age like humans. He looked a lot like me, actually. He could've been my much older brother. Not as many zits as me, though. That must be a preteen thing as opposed to a warlock thing.

"You're late," he said. He didn't move aside. Instead, he made me stand in the doorway. He liked it when I showed fear. But I wasn't about to give him the satisfaction.

"I slipped in the hall," I said. This wasn't a lie. The stupid giant slugs had slimed up the halls so badly that everybody was tripping over themselves between classes.

"Yes, I suppose we should do something about all that slug slime," he said, smiling. Most people looked nicer when they smiled. Not Master Dreadthorn. It made him look even more menacing.

"Is that my punishment, then? Cleaning slug slime?" I asked, almost relieved to get off so easily. I knew a great spell for cleaning up slime. Chad taught it to me. In addition to baking spells, he was also great at cleaning spells. We had the cleanest room in the dormitories. Beyond that, Chad pretty much reeked at Spelling.

"No, I think we'll save slug slime for someone who wasn't drawing cartoons during my lecture," he said, stepping aside and motioning for me to come in. Drat.

He stopped behind an imposing desk, the top of which was an enormous slab of black onyx stone. On it were various teacher things: some leaves of parchment, a few books and ink and a quill. There were also stranger things, like a jar with eyeballs floating in some kind of gelatinous fluid, a deathwatch beetle ticking down the time to somebody's death, and a human skull that was currently doing double duty as a candleholder.

A quick glance around the study revealed dark, cobwebby shelves spilling over with dusty spell books, charms, and jars. The room was lit mostly by candles, although an eerie red glow always emanated from the

Dread Master's crystal ball, which was locked in a glass case behind his desk. There were no windows, as we were underground. Yet, somehow, the night seemed to seep in, filling cracks and corners with its inky presence.

"You've been having problems in class, Rune," Master Dreadthorn said. I was still standing even though there was a leather chair next to me. I hadn't been invited to sit. And it didn't really look like I was going to be anytime soon.

"You can't really qualify doodling as 'problems,'" I answered. That was stupid. Why couldn't I just keep my big mouth shut?

Master Dreadthorn glared at me with his dead, black shark eyes.

"No, I don't suppose," he answered in a cool, even tone. "However," he said, pulling out a few leaves of parchment. I recognized them at once as the notes my other Masters had given me. They were supposed to be handed to a parent. Of course, I had just hidden them under my bed. It wasn't really the most original hiding place. Still, I wondered how the Dread Master had gotten his hands on them.

"Your other instructors are also having problems with you, Rune. Problems that go beyond mere doodling." He shuffled through the pile. "Master Igor said you warned a fellow classmate of an attack during a sneaking exercise."

Master Igor was our Stealthmaster. In his class, we learned how to be secretive, sneaky, and sly—all the traits of a Master villain.

"That exercise wasn't even fair. Igor pitted the hoofed kids against the padfooted kids. I was just evening the odds."

"And here," Master Dreadthorn continued, unimpressed, "Mistress Helga writes that you shielded a girl during weapons training."

"It was Jezebel . . . uh . . . that is . . . the countess. We were throwing wooden stakes. She's a vampire. Someone could've gotten hurt." I was starting to sound like Chad.

"Enough. Rune, you are not taking your villain training seriously. You are twelve years old. Almost all the other kids in your age group have advanced to Fiend Level or beyond. You're still a Rogue, for badness' sake!"

That kind of stung. Mostly because it was true. We didn't progress through grades at Master Dreadthorn's School for Wayward Villains (like kindergarten, first, second). Instead, we had achievement levels called Educational Villain Levels (or EViLs). The first level was Crook. The second, Rogue. Then Fiend, Apprentice, and finally, Master.

"Master Stiltskin says I could be Fiend Level in Spelling," I said on the defensive.

"That's because Stiltskin's a softhearted fool. He's as much a villain as Little Bo Peep was." I couldn't really argue with that. I loved Master Stiltskin, but he was a total softie. And with my Spelling skills (or lack thereof) I barely merited Rogue Level, let alone *Fiend* Level.

"It's time for you to be challenged, Rune. Intelligence isn't your problem. It's discipline. You get bored. You're not one of those villains who likes to plot in dark corners; you're more suited for fieldwork."

I perked up at the mention of *fieldwork.*

"It's time for you to have a Plot. And I've already got a few things in mind. I think this will be just the kind of challenge you need to whip you into shape. If you succeed, you'll advance to Fiend."

Sweet, I thought. I came expecting slug slime and ended up with my very own Plot!

"But . . . ," Master Dreadthorn continued. Oh, no. Heavy, ominous *but*s were never good. (Orksy Toren— that troll kid—could attest to that. He had to endure a heavy butt for three hours.)

"But?" I asked.

"If you fail in this Plot, you will be exiled. Cast from the school and hunted by both villain and hero alike."

Then Master Dreadthorn smiled a truly evil, villainous smile. I knew then that my exile was exactly what he anticipated. I was a thorn in his side, an embarrassment, and he had found a way to successfully rid himself of me once and for all. What a jerk. What a scoundrel. What a villain! I couldn't help admiring the old man even as I loathed him.

* * *

"A Plot?" Chad asked after I returned to our dorm. "What is it?" He sounded fascinated and also a little frightened.

"I don't know yet," I answered. "He said a messenger would bring it to me this week. But that's not even the best part. If I succeed, Master D. says I'll make Fiend Level!"

"No way!" Chad said.

He was hanging over the top bunk of the bed. I was sitting below him, biting off gingerbread heads just to watch the frosting ooze out. Chad was one of the few kids my age who hadn't reached Fiend Level yet either. "No more scullery duty!" he said.

Some kids were naturally motivated to rise in their villain levels. After all, ambition and greed are common villain traits. However, some of us need more motivating. So the lowest levels were given the foulest chores to do until they reached a new level. The chores became less and less revolting until one achieved Master Level. Then the villain graduated and went out into the world to pursue his or her evil interests—or in the case of the school Masters, stayed at school to teach.

The lowest level, Crooks, got bathroom duty. They were also pretty much slaves to the rest of us—forced to do the bidding of advanced-level kids until they reached Rogue. Then it was kitchen duty . . . peeling potatoes, scrubbing pots and pans. I hated that.

"Fiend Level would be nice," I said. And I meant it. As a Fiend, all I had to do was some light dusting and feed the animals we kept for Spelling and PE (Potion Extracting, not Physical Education—although gathering dragon fire to light the hall torches would *definitely* count as Physical Education).

"I wonder if anyone will get to Plot with you," Chad said. He tried to sound casual, but I could hear the eagerness in his voice. He was sick of being Rogue Level too.

"If I get to choose someone, I'll ask for you," I said.

It was a total lie. No way was I letting a screwup like Chad ruin my one chance to prove myself to Master Dreadthorn. I mean, I liked the guy okay, but seriously? Inviting Chad to Plot would be like inviting Dracula to tea. It just wouldn't work.

"Really? Thanks, man!" he said, oblivious.

I was completely confident. Books and classes really weren't my thing. I craved action. There was nothing that could stop me from reaching Fiend Level. Then, two days later, my Plot arrived.

* * *

The school day (or in this case, night) started with the official announcement of the full moon field trip to Mistress Morgana's School for Exemplary Villains. Then the big news:

"As all of you know, this is the harvest moon," a tinny voice echoed from a hole in the wall. A network of hollowed-out holes connected to the school office, where Miss Salem—a hag—read the announcements each morning. "In celebration of the harvest moon, names will be drawn by lottery for participation in a Plot of the Master and Mistress Villains' choosing. If your name is drawn, you will be excused from class responsibilities for the duration. Participation in the Plot is mandatory. You will be expected to scheme, connive, and conspire until the Plot is completed or upon your failure or demise."

A series of cheers could be heard throughout the dungeons. That was until Miss Salem announced that supper would be raw sheep liver, spinach (thanks to

Ivan's jolly green dad), mac and cheese, and a choice of chocolate milk or blood to drink. It was impossible to please so many different breeds of villains, so meals usually consisted of a wide variety. But no matter what kind of villain, kids were mostly grossed out by the spinach.

At supper, Chad and I sat at a table with Wolf Junior, Jezebel, and a few other villains our age. I traded Wolf most of my sheep liver for his mac and cheese. Jez tried to talk me into giving her a sip of my chocolate milk. She still wasn't keen on a vampire diet, but she always took the blood to keep up appearances. Chad—being a total freak—actually traded a bunch of his gingerbread men for everybody's spinach.

"They would've just given it to you, man," I said.

Chad shrugged. "I've got lots of gingerbread. So, any word about you-know-what?" he asked with an overkill of winking and nudging.

"What?" Jezebel asked. "What's he mean?"

"Can I tell her?" Chad asked.

"Tell her what?" Wolf Junior chimed in.

All three of them were leaning toward me, eyes wide, mouths open. It was perfect.

"Nah, they're not interested," I said, hiding a smile.

"Rune!" all three of them said together.

"Geez. It's no big deal," I said, but I really hoped Chad

would spill the beans. Getting my own Plot was just too cool to keep secret. Everyone would be so jealous.

"Rune's dad is giving him a Plot," Chad squeaked like a girl.

"No way!" Jez and Wolf said in unison. Little flecks of sheep liver landed in my mac and cheese from Wolf's stupid, lolling dog tongue.

"Gross!" I said, picking them out. "Say it, don't spray it, Wolf!"

"Rorry," he said through another mouthful of sheep liver.

"So, uh, is anybody . . . you know . . . Plotting with you?" Jez asked. She tucked her hands under her chin and tilted her head, batting her lashes at me.

"Yeah," Wolf Junior said, assuming the same girly pose and talking in a high-pitched voice, "because you're so *dreeeeamy*, Rune."

Jezebel's face went from sweet to scary as she turned and hissed at Wolf.

"He doesn't know yet," Chad answered for me. "Besides, if he does get to choose somebody, it'll be me."

"No way he'd choose you over me, right, Rune?" Jez said.

"Wait, don't I get to go?" Wolf asked.

They all looked at me. Luckily the bell rang, and I dashed out before things got ugly.

In the hallway after school dismissed, all the kids buzzed and gossiped about the upcoming field trip. Who would be chosen for the Plot? What would it be? But I hardly cared anymore. After all, I had a Plot of my own.

I ran into Chad on the way down to the kitchen, where we would wash dishes with the other Rogues. Just as we were descending the stone steps leading to the cafeteria, a cat-a-bat landed on my shoulder, digging its claws into my flesh. Cat-a-bats look like cats, only smaller, with bat wings, forked tongues, and elongated fangs. They're almost always black, except for an occasional freak calico. I was drawing one in my dad's class the day I got busted.

Anyway, cat-a-bats were useful for sending villain messages, and I knew this one. She belonged to Master Dreadthorn. Her name was Tabs. Dad sometimes used her to spy on people. I think that's where the phrase "I'm keeping Tabs on you" came from.

"Ouch, Tabs!" I said. "Do you mind? My shoulder is still bleeding from your last visit."

Tabs retracted her claws, and I reached up to her fanged mouth, where she held a black envelope delicately between her sharp teeth.

"This is it," I told Chad, who just stared in awe.

I reached into my pocket for a chunk of sheep liver

I'd saved from supper just for this purpose and handed it to Tabs. She perched on my shoulder, munching and purring, then licked her paws and flew off.

"Aren't you gonna open it?" Chad asked. Other Rogues were filing past us into the kitchen; some had noticed Tabs and the letter.

"Not until later, when we're alone," I said, tucking the letter beneath my velvet cloak.

I'd never washed dishes so quickly in my life. My speed was only slightly slower than Chad's, who was an exemplary dishwasher under normal circumstances (it went along with baking and cleaning skills, I suppose). He finished his own chores, then helped me finish up mine. Once Cook—an old, gnarled, one-eyed pirate—approved our work, we were dashing off to our dormitory. We rounded a slippery corner, lost our footing, and nearly tripped over a couple Crooks who were scrubbing slug slime in our hallway. Neither one of them looked older than six or seven.

"Watch it, Crooks!" Chad said, kicking one of them in the shin. The kid bit back tears. I stared at Chad in wonder.

"I don't think I've ever seen you be mean to anyone . . . ever," I said. Being cruel kind of came with villain territory. Some of us were meaner than others. But Chad? I didn't think he had it in him.

He just shrugged and dashed down the hall into

our room. I lingered behind just for a minute, made sure nobody was watching, then handed the kids a couple of Chad's gingerbread men I had stashed in my cloak pocket.

"They bleed when you bite their heads," I said, smiling.

"Cool!" the Crooks said.

The littler one wiped his sleeve across his wet cheeks and smiled at me. Hey, I couldn't have them crying all over the place. It might make the halls more slippery than the slug slime. I mean, I wasn't just being nice. Villains are *not* nice to children. We even had to watch a short film about it last year titled, *Silly Villain! Kids Are for Snacks!*

Finally, I reached my dorm and shut the door. Chad was practically bouncing on the top of his bunk bed in anticipation.

"Open it, Rune!" he said.

"Okay, okay." I reached into my cloak and pulled out the black envelope. On it, written in silver ink, were two words: Rune Drexler.

I tore open the envelope and pulled out the parchment. I read as I unfolded it:

Plot for Rune Drexler, Rogue:
You are to complete the following tasks within <u>*one week*</u>*, that is seven days, after the night of the*

harvest moon. Should you fail in even <u>one</u> of these tasks, you will be immediately exiled from Master Dreadthorn's School for Wayward Villains. If you succeed, you will achieve the rank of Fiend.

I was so excited; I could hardly make my fingers unfold the rest of the parchment. What would it be? Stealing jewels? Causing an earthquake? My eyes skimmed down the page.

"What!" I shouted.

"What is it, Rune?" Chad asked.

"I don't believe this. It's not possible."

"What?" Chad was practically salivating.

I read aloud, "'Number one, kidnap a princess. Number two, steal a baby. Number three, find a hench-man and commit him to your service . . .'"

"That's not so bad," Chad said, although he didn't sound too sure.

"I've saved the best for last," I said, growing a little hysterical. "'Number four, overthrow a kingdom and place a ruler of your choice on the throne.'"

"Well . . . uh . . . that's . . ."

"Impossible!" I said. "I'm supposed to do all that in *seven days*! I can't do it." My toes felt numb. My eye began to twitch. Slowly, I forced myself to calm down. To think.

"Maybe I can combine some of this. You know? Maybe I can . . . uh . . . steal a baby princess and make her my henchman?"

"Uh . . . I guess that could work." Chad didn't look convinced.

"I'm dead." My eye twitched as I spoke.

Chad just stared at me with pity.

At the bottom of the note a few more words were written. I didn't dare share them with Chad, knowing the consequences if I did. Still, I clung to that little sentence like a lifeline in a turbulent sea:

You may choose two Conspirators to Plot with you.

CHAPTER THREE

Another Plot

It's funny how a lecture on the history of villainy can make the time go so slowly. Yet, imminent death just speeds the old clock right up.

The night of the harvest moon arrived, and I was a mess. I still had no idea how to accomplish my Plot. I pulled on my boots only to realize they were on the wrong feet. I gave up and just stared blankly at my hands. From across the room, I dimly noticed Chad watching me with concern. He had finally stopped trying to cheer me up with his latest invention: cookies that bite back.

When the Great Clock chimed the hour, I jumped and turned my head nervously from side to side before slumping over and staring at my hands once more.

"Uh, Rune," Chad said. "We have to assemble with everyone outside. For the field trip. Remember?"

"Field trip?" I asked, unsure where I was.

"To Morgana's? They're drawing for the Plot tonight, and—"

"Plot? *Plot!*" I shouted.

At the sound of the *P*-word my eye twitched like crazy. I pressed both hands on it, coming back to my senses a little. I could see Chad had backed up to a wall and was eyeing the doorway nervously.

"Sorry," I said. "Let's go."

I followed Chad into the hallway, where students were already elbowing and jostling each other on their way to the school entrance. Everyone spilled out of the narrow hallway and into the darkness of the night.

The entire school was located under the ruins of an old castle. It consisted of a series of underground tunnels, dungeons, and caves. The land—a blackened, nearly sunless waste—had been donated to the school by Jezebel's dad, Dracula. She was always such a brat about how her dad had paid for this and that and he was oh-so-important.

In the moonlight, I could see Master Dreadthorn and a handful of other teachers standing at the front of the mob. Master Stiltskin caught my eye and smiled his sunken, toothless old-man grin, waving one bony hand at me, but I hardly took notice. Instead, I stood stoically as a rumbling sound grew louder and louder, and a caravan of Gypsy wagons materialized from the darkness. The colorful wagons, adorned with brightly dyed cloth and fluttering flags, came to a crunching halt at the school entrance.

Master Dreadthorn eyed the vibrant wagons with thinly veiled revulsion.

"I thought I told you to dial it down, Ursus," the Dread Master said to the driver. "We have an image to maintain, you know."

"I did dial it down," the burly driver said in a low, rumbling voice.

Master D. and the driver glared at each other, and for a moment I thought the field trip might end then and there. But the Dread Master, his eyes still on the monstrous form of Ursus, lifted a hand, motioning for everyone to load up.

I was still mostly out of it as the impossibility of my Plot wormed its way once more into my thoughts. I got into a wagon with Chad, Jezebel, Wolf, and a few other kids I didn't really know. The other students piled into the rest of the wagons. After a few skirmishes (and one serious vampire bite) the caravan rumbled forward, and we were on our way.

Some of the kids in our wagon talked about their excitement over the Plot. This sent me into another panic, and my hand flew up to my eye to still the spasms. Chad edged away from me.

"What's wrong with him?" Wolf Junior asked.

"He got his Plot," Chad said. "It's not good."

"Really?" Jezebel asked. "Tell us about it!"

Chad took one look at me and my twitching eye and said, "Maybe later."

It took about an hour for us to arrive at a port where Cook's pirate ship—*The Horrid Knave*—was docked, waiting to carry us down the coast to Mistress Morgana's snobby school. I'd spent the entire trip in silence, contemplating my terrible Plot.

"Uh, Rune?" It was Jezebel.

"Uh-huh?" I asked. My eye had never stopped twitching.

"We have to get on the ship, Rune," she said. I didn't respond.

"Is it really *that* bad?" Wolf asked Chad.

"Yeah," he said, throwing one of my arms across his shoulders, "it is."

Vaguely, I registered the fact that my friends were hauling me out of the wagon and up a wooden plank onto *The Horrid Knave*. A motley crew of Cook's scalawags manned the sails. I could hear a slow, steady chant rising from below deck that would allow the rowers to keep the ship moving steadily down the coast. Then there was rocking. Then there was puking. (Did I mention I get a little seasick?)

31

Then I was walking back down a plank and onto dry land again.

I didn't really come to my senses until we arrived at Mistress Morgana's. I'd been there before, but my memory never did the place justice. It was a towering medieval castle complete with gargoyles and a moat—the place was a villain's dream! Even as we approached, a drawbridge was being lowered.

I wondered how Morgana got away with having so many windows until we crossed the bridge and I realized they were all heavily curtained with black velvet. We mounted the expansive stone steps, and the entire student body sprawled on the landing. In the distance, I could hear the eerie, mournful howling of the werewolf students as they transformed beneath the full moon. Then Master Dreadthorn swept past with a swirling of his dark cloak.

One of the Crooks, a troll, was whining about being hungry. As Master Dreadthorn passed he "accidentally" knocked the Crook off the landing and into the moat. After grappling with the moat monster—which was a kind of giant squid—the poor kid hauled himself up the shore, dripping with foul mucky water and shooting a scathing look at Master D.

The Dread Master didn't even break stride as he marched purposefully up to the double oak doors.

He'd just raised his hand to the enormous iron knocker when the door opened and a woman stepped out to greet us.

I'd seen her before on our last visit, but I'd forgotten how gorgeous Morgana was. Her lips were bloodred, her hair was long and blond, and she wore this green sparkly dress that matched the shade of her catlike eyes.

"Welcome, my dear Veldin!" she said in a British accent, opening her arms to invite us all in.

"I prefer *Master Dreadthorn*, if you don't mind," he said stiffly, brushing past Morgana. The rest of us shuffled in behind. I noticed immediately that the Morgana students were nowhere to be found.

I was about to mention this to the others but didn't get a chance because Morgana was organizing everyone for a tour. This was mostly for the Crooks who hadn't been to Mistress Morgana's school before. We started in the entrance hall, where portraits of famous alumni hung on the walls. She named them off for us, as if we hadn't studied them in Dad's history class. He looked even more offended than the rest of us.

"And this," Morgana said, pointing to an enormous painting of Jezebel's dad, "is our dear friend Count Dracula. I believe his niece or someone like that goes to your school, Veldin?" she asked.

"I'm his *daughter!*" Jezebel answered. I could tell that Morgana had known that perfectly well.

"Of course you are, dear. Of course. I'm just a little surprised that a villain as great as Dracula would have a daughter at a school for *wayward* villains," Morgana answered. I thought I saw Jezebel's cheeks flush, which was pretty weird considering she didn't have a heartbeat.

Master Dreadthorn narrowed his eyes as Morgana went on and on about how she and the count (Dracula) were *such good friends*. As far as villains go, the count was at the top of the list. Plus he was rich. He donated gold to both villain schools, but the fact that the count adored Morgana and pretty much ignored Master Dreadthorn didn't do much for my dad's feelings toward Morgana. He loathed the woman.

"My dad went here," Wolf Junior piped up. "But I don't see his picture on the wall."

Morgana wrinkled her nose as if Wolf smelled bad (which he kind of did, but it still wasn't very nice). "We only hang portraits of *important* alumni," she answered curtly. "I don't believe eating pork and scaring little girls in red capes really qualifies someone."

Wolf growled.

By the time we'd climbed up and down a gazillion steps and met all the teachers, I was famished. So famished, in fact, that I'd nearly forgotten my Plot. Then we arrived back at the entrance, where tables had been set up, but instead of food, they were filled with flickering lanterns.

"It's such a lovely night," Morgana said. "Let's take a stroll."

Everyone groaned loudly at the idea of walking around outside. However, one look from Dreadthorn and most of the students were smart enough to shut up—except one. The stupid troll Crook hadn't even dried yet when the Dread Master hoisted him up by the back of his cloak, carried him outside, and flung him back into the moat. Some kids never learn.

Morgana and Master Dreadthorn each picked up a lantern and motioned for us to do the same.

"This way," Morgana said.

We followed them back outside, where a dark trail disappeared into a dense wood. The troll kid sloshed along beside us—silent now—as we followed the path beneath the skeletal trees.

"Are we there yet?" Wolf muttered next to me. "I'm starved."

"Yeah, I could do with a bite myself," Jezebel said. She turned to look at me in an appraising sort of way.

"Don't even think about it," I said, eyeing her nervously.

"What?" she asked innocently. "I was just going to ask if you had any chocolate on you."

"Here." Chad passed out a few gingerbread men to tide us over. We had to cover their mouths to muffle the screams so the Dread Master wouldn't catch us snacking.

On we trudged for what seemed like an eternity. The fall evening had turned cool beneath the orange glow of the harvest moon.

The sound of teeth chattering came from somewhere nearby, and I thought it must be the troll kid. I was about to tell him off when I realized it was Chad, cowering in fear next to me and jumping every time a branch snapped or an owl hooted.

"Don't be a baby. You're embarrassing yourself," I said, even as I pulled my cloak tighter. I mean, *I* wasn't afraid or anything. Villains *do not* get afraid walking through dark, disturbing woods with tree-bark eyes and scratchy leaf voices and groping, gnarled branch-hands. I was just *cold*.

Finally, we emerged from the woods and into a well-lit clearing. I sighed with relief as the feeling of dread . . . uh . . . *cold* faded. Before us stretched an enormous black swamp and six ultralong tables that had been set with china plates, fine silverware, and elaborate centerpieces.

"Ah! He must have known I'd be here. Why else would he go to such trouble?" Jez said, looking particularly haughty.

"What are you talking about?" I asked.

She gestured to the decorations.

All around the clearing, skulls had been set on spikes with little flickering candles inside them, making the empty eye sockets glow. I also noticed skulls on the tables, hollowed out like bowls and containing various exotic foods. It looked *expensive*—and slightly repulsive.

Most of Master Dreadthorn's students were staring with their mouths open like a bunch of slobbering morons. Morgana looked smugly satisfied. And now I could see what Jez had been talking about. Black cards had been placed on every table. An elegant silver script announced:

The harvest moon festivities, provisions,
table service, and skulls were made possible by
a generous donation from Count Dracula.

"Uh, Jez," Wolf said, "I'm not sure all this is for you."

"What?" she asked dangerously.

"I don't think your dad—ouch!"

I pinched Wolf and whispered, "Let. It. Go. Do you *see* her face?"

We both turned to see Jez baring her teeth at us.

"Never mind," Wolf said.

Standing to either side of the tables were the students of Mistress Morgana's. I'd forgotten they were required to wear uniforms here. They looked like rows of toy soldiers. The boys wore black trousers, white shirts, black cloaks, and funny little velvet berets. The girls wore similar outfits, only with skirts instead of pants. This worked for most of the kids, but the trolls, giants, and other non-humans (who were usually clad in cut-offs or loincloths) looked positively ridiculous.

Morgana's school used the same Educational Villain Levels as our school. I could see the poor Crooks balancing heavy trays of food and standing by to wait on the others. They had no berets at all. The rest of the ranks were sorted by hat color. Green for Rogues, blue for Fiends, red for Apprentices, and the school Masters wore gold, except for Mistress Morgana. Apparently, the dress code didn't apply to her.

Morgana made her way between the rows of tables, with Master Dreadthorn next to her. We all followed gracelessly behind in no particular order. I noticed that as Morgana passed, her perfect rows of students bowed in unison.

"Suck-ups," I said under my breath. "I'm glad we don't have to wear stuff like that."

"I dunno, Rune," Wolf said, nodding toward my dad.

I could see the way the Dread Master's eyes flicked from Morgana's orderly rows to his own unorganized mob. I worried that changes might be coming for the students of Master Dreadthorn's School for Wayward Villains—changes involving berets and color coordination.

No tables had been designated for us. Apparently, we were supposed to mingle with Morgana's students. Luckily, I managed to find a place with extra openings, so Jezebel, Chad, and Wolf all sat with me. Across from us, Morgana's students were still standing, their tidy cloaks fluttering in the cool night breeze.

"What are they waiting for?" Jez whispered to me. I just shrugged.

Morgana stopped at the head of all the tables, where a platform had been raised with a special table for the teachers. She stood next to Master Dreadthorn, whose black eyes seemed to burn with a variety of emotions. I was pretty sure I saw anger, embarrassment, and jealousy, to name a few.

"Be seated," Morgana said in her tinkling voice.

Her students sat as one. Then the Crooks brought

out the food and stood obediently near the trees, waiting to refill drinks or to pick up dropped napkins. Whenever a Crook was slow (or even if one was too attentive), he or she was given demerits—which meant extra cleaning duties on top of all the Crook's regular chores. Apparently, *anyone* ranking above a Crook at Morgana's school could give them demerits, not just the Masters. So the poor kids were heaped with indignities as the older generation sought to take petty revenge for the years *they'd* spent as Crooks.

I thought I saw them watching our own Crooks with longing. The rest of Morgana's students, however, stared down their pointy noses at us like we were left-over sheep liver.

"So," a girl across from us said. I could tell she was a Fiend by her hat color. I could tell she was a vampire by her features. "Is it true you have to do something *good* to get into Dreadthorn's?"

"I guess," Jezebel answered, since the girl seemed to be talking to her.

"What did *you* do?" she asked.

"Uh . . . I don't really like to talk about it," Jez said. She'd been drinking grape juice and trying to pass it off as blood in the dim candlelight. She eyed her glass nervously.

"I heard what she did," another kid piped up. It was

a boy a few seats down from us. He might have been a warlock like me. "My dad hangs around in the same cave as her dad sometimes. Anyway, turns out Little Miss Dracula likes chocolate milk," he said in a mocking voice.

"It was hot cocoa," Jez said, staring at her plate.

"Gross!" the girl across from us said. "No wonder your dad disowned you."

"He did *not* disown me! In fact, he donated the land for Master Dreadthorn's school."

"He donated land for our school too. Hmm . . . a wasteland and a dungeon for his daughter, and a castle on the sea for perfect strangers. Sounds like your dad doesn't really care about you, kiddo."

This was hardly true since Dracula was immortal and had donated the land about three hundred years before Jezebel was even born. On the other hand, he really was a jerk to Jezebel most of the time, so the vampire girl did have a point.

"That's not true!" Jez said, but they'd already moved on.

"What about you, dog-boy?" the warlock kid asked. "Did your dad really dress up like a little old grandma?" Everyone at the table giggled.

"It was a disguise!" Wolf Junior said.

"But *Grandmama*," the vampire girl said. "What a

big hairy *butt* you have!" Now the whole table erupted in laughter.

"Just ignore them," I said. Chad and I were both holding Wolf Junior back by his tail as he tried to scramble across the table.

"Down, boy!" the girl said. "If you can sit, I'll give you a nice biscuit. Sit boy. Sit!" More laughter.

"Shouldn't you be howling at the moon with the other dogs?" the boy asked.

"I'm not a werewolf, moron!" Wolf said.

"You look like one to me," the vampire girl said, smirking.

"Werewolves *transform*. He's always like that," Chad added helpfully. Only it wasn't really very helpful.

Wolf Junior was about to pounce on Little Miss Snot Nose when Mistress Morgana lifted her crystal goblet and spoon, clinking them for everyone's attention. The tables grew silent.

"We are so pleased to have our friends from Master Dreadthorn's School for Wayward Villains here tonight." A round of halfhearted clapping echoed dully from the tables and was lost in the stillness of the night.

"We are also excited because—as all of you know—this is the month of the harvest moon. And that means

42

we will once again be drawing names for a very secret, very dangerous Plot!"

The clapping this time was thunderous. There was even shouting and a few whistles. Then, two beefy men in black hoods entered the clearing from the far end carrying an enormous metal cauldron between them. As they made their way between the tables, a low chant began, growing louder and louder.

"Plot! Plot! Plot! Plot!"

I felt a familiar twinge in my eye as I was reminded once more of my own terrible Plot. But I couldn't afford to freak out now with the Morgana kids watching. Besides, my mind had finally cleared a little and my villain instincts were taking over. I knew what I had to do. If I could get Jez and Wolf alone for a minute—

Somebody banged the table so hard, my fork flew into my lap. Kids were no longer just chanting, they were screaming.

"Plot! Plot! Plot! Plot!"

It echoed from the surrounding trees. More kids pounded their fists on the tables in rhythm. The chanting grew to a climax as the two headsmen climbed the steps to the platform where Mistress Morgana and Master Dreadthorn waited.

The chanting voices and fist-pounding were so

43

loud now, even the ground seemed to be shaking. Mistress Morgana held up her hands for silence, and immediately the noise stopped. It was like the final drumbeat of a song. The sound echoed around and around the clearing, dying to a whisper and disappearing into the night air.

"This cauldron contains the names of every eligible student from both my school and Veldin's school," Morgana said.

I saw my father's mouth move. Although I couldn't hear what he said, I was pretty sure it looked like *"Master Dreadthorn*, you dimwit."

Morgana had said *every eligible student*. That probably didn't include Crooks or kids failing their classes. I wondered if I was eligible even though I already had a Plot. An impossible, horrible one. My eye twitched again.

"Three names will be chosen by an *impartial* party," Morgana continued. "If your name is called, please stand and join me and Veldin on the platform."

I had just enough time to wonder who the "impartial party" would be when the two burly men tipped the enormous cauldron, dumping the names into the swamp. Immediately, the surface of the water began to bubble. All of the kids rushed from the tables and down to the waterside to get a better view. Wolf, Jez,

Chad, and I elbowed our way to the front, accidentally bumping the troll Crook into the water for the third time that night. He emerged, soggy and dripping, just as the swamp changed from an inky black to an eerie, glowing green.

"Lady of the Lake, Maiden of the Mire," Morgana said, "choose the names of those who will conspire."

A bony hand shot out of the lake, clutched in a tight fist. Bits of decayed gray flesh hung limply from it like an old, tattered flag. This was all that was left of the original Lady of the Lake. Apparently, Morgana had held a grudge against the woman back in England (something about the Lady giving Arthur a sword one Christmas when all Morgana got from her was a lame pair of reindeer socks). She enslaved the Lady, banishing her to this swamp where the quagmire had eventually rotted her body away, leaving just the hand behind.

Beside me I could see Chad's eyes open wide in awe at the sight of the grisly hand. Wolf had momentarily forgotten his quarrel with the vampires. His tongue lolled as he panted madly in anticipation. Jez had her hands squeezed into fists and her eyes shut tight as she chanted under her breath, "Countess Jezebel, Countess Jezebel, oh *please* Countess Jezebel."

The Morgana kids were taking a more proactive

approach. I could hear more than one student quietly muttering cheating spells. Morgana reached out her fingers to delicately pluck the name from the gruesome hand. The entire assembly was silent, everyone collectively holding their breath.

"The first to Plot shall be . . ." Morgana met the eyes of all the students, purposefully keeping us in suspense. Villains love suspense.

"Erzsebet Bathory!" Morgana announced, holding the little metal nameplate high over her head.

"Who is that?" Wolf Junior asked.

"Me, dogbreath," a girl said.

It was the vampire who'd been taunting us. She smiled, showing her long, venomous fangs. The girl held up her pale hand amid cheers from her fellow students and strode gracefully toward Morgana. Judging by the thunderous applause, it was obvious Erzsebet was popular.

After the noise quieted down, Morgana said her rhyme again. The bony hand plunged back beneath the lake where the water boiled, still glowing green. Moments later, the hand emerged with another name.

"The second to Plot shall be . . ." Again a long pause.

"Morgana's such a drama queen," I said.

"Shhh!" several people nearby hissed at me.

Beside me Jez was nearly hyperventilating from

chanting her own name. On the other side, Wolf was still clutching his plate in one hand and a raw mutton leg in the other. He had left a puddle of drool on his dinner plate from panting. A Crook noticed at the same time I did and rushed forward to wipe it up.

"Gilles DeRay!" Morgana announced.

Another vampire held up his hand near the other end of the crowd, also one of Mistress Morgana's snobs. He joined Erzsebet on the platform. Mistress Morgana was about to say her rhyme for the third and final time when Master Dreadthorn cleared his throat meaningfully.

"I'd like to do it this time if you don't mind," he said.

For a brief moment, Mistress Morgana's flawless control faltered. Her eyes hardened, turning the liquid green light into two solid emeralds. Then she regained her composure and stepped aside gracefully.

The Dread Master said the rhyme in a bored sort of voice that revealed his distaste for anything singsongy. The skeletal hand dived once more beneath the churning surface of the swamp only to emerge moments later.

Master Dreadthorn plucked the name from the hand and looked at it for a good thirty seconds. His face betrayed nothing, but I could tell he was calculating in his mind. He obviously recognized the name, so I figured it must be from our school. I only hoped it wasn't mine. Finally, Master Dreadthorn's dead, black eyes fell on us as he said, "Chad Padurii."

CHAPTER FOUR

Conspiracies

Poor Chad froze on the spot. For a minute, I thought he was going to pee his pants. Or maybe his head would just fall off and he'd ooze red frosting like one of his gingerbread men.

"It's you, Chad," I said helpfully. No response. I pinched him.

"Ouch!" he said, coming out of his trance. Slowly, he walked in a daze toward the platform.

"We have our Conspiracy!" Morgana said.

The water stopped boiling as the hand disappeared. The lake was black once more. Everyone clapped, although most kids looked downcast. It was more fun to be in the parade than to watch it from the sidelines. But the disappointment on my friends' faces made me hopeful. And now that Chad had his own Plot, I wouldn't even have to feel guilty. Guilt was *not* a good villain trait. It implied a conscience—definitely something villains should not have.

I had to start my own Plot in the morning, which meant I only had tonight to convince Wolf and Jezebel to join my Conspiracy. When we returned to the castle, the chosen Plotters disappeared into a private room with Morgana and Dreadthorn. The rest of us kids were dismissed to roam the castle and grounds until midnight. I took advantage of the opportunity and managed to get Wolf and Jezebel alone in a spare room.

"I can't believe *Chad* is Plotting and not us," Wolf said as I closed the door behind us. They hardly realized I'd herded them into a separate room.

"I know. What's *he* going to do on a Plot?" Jez said. "Bake a mighty cake of destruction?"

"Guys," I said.

"Whip up a headless gingerbread army?" Wolf said.

"Guys!"

"Stir up a—" Jez began.

"GUYS!" I shouted. They finally stopped ranting long enough to notice me.

"What, Drexler?" Wolf asked.

"How'd you like to Plot with me?" I said.

"Seriously?" Jez asked.

I pulled out my Plot message and read it to them

just like I had to Chad. Only this time, I included the part at the bottom . . . that I was allowed to choose two Conspirators.

"That sounds kind of hard. No wonder you were freaked out," Wolf said.

"I wasn't freaked out!"

"Oh yeah? What about all that . . . ?" Wolf twitched his eye at me.

"You want an eye twitch, Junior? I'll give you one!" I said.

"What about Chad?" Jez said, moving quickly between me and Wolf. "He said you were Plotting with him."

"Chad? Seriously?" I asked. "Besides, he has his own Plot now."

"So . . . you want *us*?" Wolf asked, somewhat surprised.

I couldn't blame him. Villain friendships were more like alliances or pacts that could be broken if they didn't prove beneficial. It was hard to tell if someone was *really* a friend or just using you.

"Think about it. If I have to kidnap a princess, steal a baby, and find a henchman . . . those are all going to require tracking. Who can track better than a wolf?"

Wolf grinned. I turned to the countess.

"And last I checked, princesses usually live in

towers. I might need someone who can fly. Plus, a bat is a lot less conspicuous than a twelve-year-old warlock, right?"

"Well, yes. My father always says I'm rather talented at stealth," Jez said (so humble).

"But what's in it for us, Rune?" Wolf asked.

"You'll share my fate. If I'm promoted to Fiend, you'll both be promoted as well," I said.

Wolf was a Rogue like me, but Jez was Fiend already. That meant an Apprentice Level for her if she succeeded. Jez was almost a year younger than me, which meant she'd become one of the youngest Apprentices ever. This would surely impress even someone as aloof as Jez's father, Count Dracula. I could see the greed gleaming in her violet eyes.

"Wait," Wolf said. "What if we fail?"

I should've lied. I should've said "No big deal, Wolfie, old boy. Nothing to worry about." Instead I told the truth.

"We're exiled," I answered.

"Forget it," Wolf and Jez both said at the same time and turned toward the door.

"Wait! Wolf, don't you want to prove to all those snobby Morgana kids that you are more than just a big dumb dog?" He stopped.

"And Jez! Wouldn't you like to prove to your dad

that you're a villain who can Plot and not just some cocoa-drinking pansy?" She stopped too.

They looked at each other. For a minute I thought they'd just walk out, but instead they both turned back to me.

"When do we start?" Jez asked.

* * *

We waited and waited for Chad to emerge from his Plotting, but he never did. Finally, the time came for us to sail back to our own school. I didn't see Chad on the boat either.

"Where's Chad?" I dared to ask Master Dreadthorn as we sailed for home.

"He's Plotting," the Dread Master answered.

I knew I wouldn't get any more than that out of him. I had to be content to assume that Chad was happily (if a bit nervously) ensconced in deep planning or, perhaps, already off on his Plot with the Morgana kids. I didn't dwell on it. After all, I had my own Plot. There was no turning back. This was my chance to prove myself to my dad once and for all. And now I had Conspirators too.

As if he'd read my mind, Master Dreadthorn asked, "Who Conspires with you?"

"Jez—uh—the countess and Wolf Junior," I answered.

The Dread Master only nodded once and said no more.

Later, after disembarking (and after cleaning up my own upchuck under the watchful eye of Cook), Jezebel, Wolf Junior, and I took advantage of the long caravan ride home to discuss where we would start our Plotting the next morning.

"There's a village some miles north of the school, past the forest," Jez said. "It borders a little kingdom called Kaloya where there's been an uprising. I heard Master Dreadthorn talking about it on the boat with Cook. Maybe it won't be so hard to overthrow a kingdom after all."

"And there's bound to be princesses and babies there," Wolf threw in. I could already tell he would be better suited as the *muscle* of this operation.

"Okay, we'll start in the village and cross over into Kaloya. Now, that just leaves finding a henchman. Jez, you said the village is north of the school, right?"

"Right."

"Okay, the road north passes through the Forgotten Forest, where there are lots of magical creatures. I've been thinking about my henchman. . . . A good henchman should be useful in some way that the villain isn't, correct?"

"Yes."

"So I was thinking, if I could find some kind of magical creature—nothing too dangerous, just something with a little bit of power—we could convince it to enter my service."

"How will we do that?" Wolf asked.

"I haven't worked that out yet," I admitted. "Maybe we can feed it the baby or something." This seemed reasonable to all of us.

"Jez, you're in charge of provisions. Fill up a few backpacks with food and supplies. And by food I mean stuff we can *all* eat."

"I'm not a bat-brain, Rune," she said.

"Could've fooled me," Wolf Junior replied. Jez bared her fangs menacingly.

"Wolf, see if you can get a map from the library."

He nodded. "What are you going to do, Rune?"

"I'm going to get us something even better than a map," I answered.

The Gypsy caravan pulled up to the school, and we got out. Jez and Wolf confirmed their responsibilities, then we all agreed to meet outside the entrance to the school at dawn. I watched them walk down the main hallway with the rest of the students, then I made my way carefully to Master Dreadthorn's study.

I was betting on the chance that he would have to talk with the Gypsies a minute or two before retiring for the day. Still, not worth risking everything on a chance. I knocked on the door. No answer. Carefully I turned the knob. It was locked, of course, but I'd stolen a spare key years ago.

The study was dark and mostly silent except for a few gurgling and scurrying noises coming from the bookshelves. The only light in the room was a red glow pulsing from the spherical object in the glass case behind Master Dreadthorn's onyx desk. His crystal ball. This, of course, was the reason I'd come here.

Wasting no time, I crossed the room to the glass case. It too was locked, but I had no key. I was certain the Dread Master would never be careless enough to leave a key in his study. After all, this *was* a school full of villains. I would have to pick the lock.

I reached into my cloak pocket and pulled out my villain tool kit—a little leather case that looked sort of like a man's wallet. Inside were various items: a few gold coins, some powders and poisons. Finally, I found what I'd been looking for: a girl's hairpin. And don't bother asking whose. That's none of your business.

With deft speed and skill, my villain's fingers made short work of the lock. In mere moments the case was open, and I was cradling the precious orb in my arms like the baby I would soon be stealing. Only I probably wouldn't be half as careful with the baby.

A search of the Dread Master's desk produced a velvet pouch. I had just deposited the orb into the pouch and pulled the drawstring tight when I heard the sound I'd been dreading . . . a key moving a tumbler, a bolt being thrown. Someone was opening the door.

I congratulated myself on remembering to lock the door behind me while at the same time scolding myself for not choosing a hiding place as soon as I had entered the room. Villains are always supposed to be on the lookout for hiding places.

There was only one substantial cover in the entire study. I dived under the onyx desk just as the door opened.

I heard a gasp and a hoarse whisper. "The crystal ball."

Oh, cat-a-bats! Any minute now, the Dread Master would come around the desk to investigate, and I'd be slug slime. If you've ever been to the principal's office for doing something bad, you might understand how I felt, but probably not. If you've ever had your dad catch you doing something you shouldn't be doing, you might also know how I felt, but again, probably not. Now, let's say your dad is a villainous warlock with a nasty temper who also *happens* to be your principal. And let's also say you're doing something that's not only bad, but pretty much illegal. And now let's say you get caught . . . doing that bad, illegal thing . . . in your dad/principal's study. Now you might know how I felt.

But the worst part is that my father would be angrier with me for getting caught than for stealing the crystal ball in the first place. Villains should *not* get caught—just ask Wolf's dad. He got caught. In a dress. By a little cape-wearing girl.

I heard another muffled gasp, then the door closing suddenly. I squeezed my eyes shut and—much like Jezebel—began chanting in my head. *Go away. Go away. Go away.* Then the sound of voices drifted in from just outside the door. Curiosity overruled my fear, and I stopped chanting long enough to listen, but the voices suddenly stopped. Then the door opened. *Again.* Back to chanting.

"Have you been waiting long?" a voice asked. I recognized it at once as the Dread Master's.

"Only a minute or two," another voice said. I nearly dropped the crystal ball from surprise. It was Chad.

"Did anybody see you?"

"No, sir."

"Well, have you formed a plan yet?" the Dread Master asked as he moved closer to the onyx desk. I heard a creaking sound and realized with growing fear that he was sitting on top of the desk, right above me.

58

"We're working on it, of course, Dread Master," Chad answered. I could hear fear in his voice, but not the usual, gibbering Chad-fear. It was more like the fear any of the students might have felt toward Master Dreadthorn. Maybe getting his own Plot had given Chad a spine.

"You'd better do more than that," Master Dreadthorn answered. "It was quite a feat for me to plant your name as the third Conspirator. For you to fail . . ."

"I won't fail you, Father," Chad answered.

This time I did drop the crystal ball. (I think this is where the phrase "drop the ball" originated.) Luckily it landed with only a faint thud, shrouded in its velvet pouch. Did he say *Father*?

"I told you never to call me *that*," the Dread Master said in a quiet, menacing way. I'd only ever seen Master Dreadthorn's anger reach this level . . . a kind of hushed smoldering that reduced students to puddles of slug slime. I would hate to see him truly angry. It would probably be the last thing I ever saw.

"Why?" Chad asked. Some of the whininess had returned to his voice. "Why does Rune get to claim you but not me? Are you still blaming me for what happened between you and Mother all those years ago?"

"Do not speak of her to me!" my father said.

"But—"

"Enough! I've allowed you to attend this school. That should be sufficient for you."

My head was reeling. Was it possible? Could Chad really be my half brother? Curly-haired, freckled, bespectacled, cookie-baking Chad? I could hardly believe it. And what did he mean about the gingerbread witch and my dad? It would take years of therapy to sort this all out, and I still had a Plot to plan and—more urgently—a crystal ball to pilfer.

"You asked me to come here in secret. And I have. Time is short. What is it you want, *Dread Master?*" Chad's voice was stiff and forceful.

"I wanted to be sure you understood your Plot," Master Dreadthorn said.

"Is that all? You mustn't believe all the rumors. I'm not as feeble-minded as everyone seems to think," Chad answered. Who *was* this brave, confident kid, and what had he done with my bumbling, shy roommate?

"That remains to be seen. And no, that is not all. I want to be sure you understand *whom* you are to establish on the throne of Kaloya."

"The girl's uncle, of course. Morgana explained everything."

Kaloya? I thought to myself. That was the kingdom my own Conspiracy was planning to overthrow. What was going on?

"By now you know of Rune's Plot?" Master Dreadthorn asked. I was surprised to hear my own name and yet, somehow, I wasn't.

"Naturally," Chad answered. "Although I don't know why you bothered placing me with Morgana's gang. You could've just given me my own Plot as you did Rune."

"You want your own Plot aside from Morgana's? Very well. I have a suspicion Rune will also travel to Kaloya. You must not let him succeed."

My eye started to twitch. I mean, I knew my father wasn't exactly the kind to take me out for ice cream or get all choked up over my first word, but *come on*! Did he really want me exiled so badly?

"Why would you want Rune to fail?" Chad asked. "It's obvious he's your favorite."

The pure jealousy in Chad's voice threw me off guard. How long had he known we were half brothers? I suddenly wondered if he'd laced my cookies with arsenic poison. It would be a very villainous thing to do. I made a mental note: if I ever got out from under this desk, I would never eat another gingerbread cookie from Chad.

"I did not say I wanted Rune to fail. I only said you must not let him succeed. A villain always has secret motives, Chad. Never forget that."

That's right. *And what exactly were the Dread Master's secret motives?* I wondered.

"How do you know he's going to Kaloya?" Chad asked.

"I saw it in the crystal," Master Dreadthorn said.

My stomach contracted and my eye twitched like a nervous cricket as I imagined Chad's gaze flickering to the empty case where my father's crystal ball had been. Any second now, and I would be discovered.

Just then I heard the Great Clock in the hall chiming the hour. It was five in the morning. Wolf and the countess would be waiting for me. I squirmed uncomfortably, pressing one hand to my wayward eye. *Rune Drexler's School for Wayward Twitching Eyes*, I thought hysterically. Despite my dire situation, I had to suppress a nervous chuckle.

"Time is short. You have but one week to complete your Plot. Don't forget what I've told you, Chad. I'll see you out."

I heard the desk creak again as the Dread Master stood. His boots landed with heavy thuds as he walked across the room. Then the door opened. Then the door closed. Then the door locked. And I was still alive.

I wasted no time. In the span of a few heartbeats I was out from under the desk, across the room, and unlocking the door. Opening it just a tiny crack, I peeked into the hall. I saw no one but faintly heard the Dread Master's steps echoing from farther down the hallway. Then the sound faded and died out.

No time to lose. I locked the door behind me and fled in the opposite direction of the ominous boot steps. I made a hasty pit stop at my dormitory. Of course, it was empty. Chad would still be with the Morgana kids, Plotting against me.

I made sure Eye of Newt had enough fire ants to last him while I was gone. He smoldered happily, crinkling his eye with pleasure. Before my stint beneath the Dread Master's desk, I might have just written a note to Chad to look after Newt if I didn't return. But not anymore.

I located my black dragonskin pack, dumped out my schoolbooks, and placed the crystal ball inside. I threw in a few changes of clothes, an extra cloak, and a variety of other things that might come in handy on a Plot, like a lantern, a blanket, a shoehorn, which, if you don't know, is a curved piece of horn (or wood or metal) used to slide a fat foot into a tiny shoe. Villains should always be prepared—a lesson from the biography of Cinderella's evil stepsisters titled *Big Feet* (not to be confused with Bigfoot's self-titled autobiography).

I'm sure you've heard the watered-down version of the tale . . . stepsisters have big feet, glass slipper doesn't fit, Cinderella gets the guy, end of story. In the *real* version, the wicked stepsisters cut off their own toes to make the shoe fit. Moral of the story: always bring a shoehorn.

Once I had packed, I turned to leave and came face-to-face with Tabs. I had to bite my tongue to hold in a scream. The black cat-a-bat hovered in the air directly in front of me with a note in her mouth. I took it, then fished around in my pocket for a sardine (having long since rid myself of the decaying sheep liver). I tossed the fish to Tabs, who watched it arc gracefully in the air and then land on the ground with a splat. Cat-a-bats were such snots. I picked it up, dusted it off, and handed it to her. She sniffed at the sardine, licked her paw, sniffed at it again, and finally took it with her tiny, pointed teeth.

"Take your time," I said sarcastically. Then I ripped open the letter.

Rune Drexler,
Do not allow Chad to complete his Plot.
Master Dreadthorn

What! I reread the note. Was he serious? I'd just heard the man telling Chad the same thing about *me*. What was he playing at? Was it some kind of test?

I didn't have time to contemplate. Instead, I shoved the letter into my cloak pocket and made my way to the school entrance. This required climbing a set of stone steps hewn from the rock of the cave floor and pulling a torch sconce that activated the Secret Mechanism.

The Secret Mechanism is the stuff of school legend.

Once the torch sconce is pulled, it lowers a weighted rope hidden behind the cave wall. This rope then pulls another rope attached to a metal foot, which kicks a chicken, which lays an egg that lands in a basket that carries it to a chute, where it slides onto the button that activates a pulley attached to a set of clockworks that roll aside a ginormous boulder that hides the school's entrance. Whew.

The entrance from the outside was also hidden. To open the boulder from the outside, one had to locate a fake rock on the ground (among the gazillion other rocks) and pull it to activate the mechanism, and the whole ridiculous thing started all over again. Once a vampire kid had gone outside, but couldn't locate the rock that opened the door. He was one of the rare, full-blooded villains. The next night, all they found of him was a charred black spot.

The entrance had been installed eons ago, back when they still taught villains that elaborate, highly involved schemes were the most likely way to ensure villainous success. However, a lot had changed in the last couple hundred years. After these complicated Plots had time and again proven disastrous, the school changed its policy on convoluted schemes. (Picture a captured hero in a villain's lair, tied up and dangling over a shark-infested lake/boiling magma/burning oil . . . you get the idea, while the villain goes on and on about his highly involved evil plan . . . giving the hero plenty of time to escape. Duh!) Since those days, our school adopted the KISS policy when it came to schemes. No, I'm not talking about saliva exchange. It stands for Keep It Simple, Stupid.

I emerged from behind the boulder to find Jez and Wolf already waiting. The sky was turning pinkish orange in the east. Jezebel's violet eyes flickered nervously toward the horizon, despite the fact she had clothed herself head to toe in a cloak with an oversized hood. She even wore gloves.

"It's about time," Wolf Junior said as I emerged.

"I ran into some trouble," I answered.

"What kind of trouble?" Jez asked, pulling her hood farther over her head.

"I'll tell you on the way. Did you get the map and the food?"

Wolf Junior and Jezebel both held up packs similar

to mine. I nodded, and turned north, with Wolf and Jez following in line behind me. Once we were safely on the road and away from the school, I told them everything I'd heard in the Dread Master's study, then I showed them the note that Tabs had brought me.

"I can't believe Chad's your brother!" Jez said.

"I can't believe he's Plotting against you!" Wolf added.

"And maybe Master Dreadthorn is too," Jez said.

This made all of us thoughtful, not to mention a little nervous, but nobody suggested that we turn back. It was too late. Once we'd decided to Plot, we had to follow through. Giving up meant failing, and failing meant exile.

CHAPTER FIVE

Into the Woods

I changed my mind. I don't want to Plot," Wolf said.

"Don't be a puppy," I said to Wolf, who had begun to whimper.

A few hours after setting off, we'd found an empty cave where we managed to catch some z's. We awoke midafternoon and continued on our way. Now, just as the sun was setting, we arrived at the threshold of a sinister place where few ventured. Magic lurked in its dark shadows, and strange, evil creatures prowled its leafy floor.

"The Forgotten Forest," Jez said in awe.

The road we were on was deserted. This was for two reasons. One, it basically ended at our school's front doorstep. Even though Master Dreadthorn kept the school mostly secret from the public, rumors were sometimes allowed to leak out. These usually involved tales of strange creatures on the road—things like vampires, wolves, and warlocks. Some people are *so* paranoid.

The other reason no one traveled this road loomed before us. As a general rule, villains enjoy dark, evil places like the forest. However, when you're not the one *making* the darkness and/or evil, it can be a little unsettling.

Just as we stepped beneath the black shadow of the trees, a piercing scream tore through the darkness. It was quickly cut off. We all eyed one another nervously.

"What do you think that was?" Wolf asked.

"Probably just an animal hunting," I said, trying to keep my cool.

The Forgotten Forest was home to a wide variety of creatures from the enormous giants to the tiny sprites— little beings like elves or leprechauns. One never knows if they are going to be helpful or jerks. It all depends on their mood swings—kind of like Jezebel.

However, as the echo of the scream faded in the distance, I wasn't worrying about *what* had caused it, but *who*. Some crafty and not-too-friendly villains had taken refuge in the Forgotten Forest. One in particular had a keen interest in stealing kids. She was called Muma Padurii, which basically means "Mother of the

Forest." She was a witch with a nasty temper. That's not really what worried me, though. The worst thing about Muma Padurii? She was Chad's mom.

Maybe you're wondering why she'd bother kidnapping kids. I mean, she already had one of her own, right? Sure, he was a cookie-baking, backstabbing pansy, but hey, he was still her son. And she must have *on some level* cared for Chad, because she sent him off to Master Dreadthorn's for an education.

Other children, however, were Muma Padurii's bread and butter. Literally. She liked to eat kids. Plus, she was still bitter about Hansel tricking her and kicking her old, wrinkly butt into the oven. She never forgot that. So, if she hated kids before, she doubly hated them now. And we were in *her* territory.

It was just after sunset, and the Forgotten Forest pressed in so closely around us, it was suffocating. A growing sense of dread descended on everyone. I kept whipping my head from side to side at every little sound. Once, I was sure I saw eyes floating in the woods just behind us, but they disappeared before I could investigate.

Wolf whimpered even louder than before. Jez was so nervous, she kept spontaneously transforming into a bat. Luckily, she'd found a spell to make her clothes transform with her, otherwise we would've been stopping every half hour to wait for her to get dressed again.

Suddenly, without warning, something shot out of the forest directly in front of us.

"Yelp!" Wolf barked in alarm.

At the same moment, Jez *popped* into a bat and tried to fly into my cloak.

"Okay! That's enough!" I yelled, turning to confront the creature that had managed to frighten three villains-in-training.

It was a rabbit. A small one.

Jez caught sight of Fluffy the Bunny and turned back into a girl. Luckily, she wasn't still in my cloak, or it might have been awkward.

"Sorry," she said.

It was obvious we were all getting just a little bit tense.

"I think we need a break," I said. "Let's stop for a bite. Jez, what did you bring?"

Jezebel rummaged through her pack and pulled out a raw steak. She tossed it into the air, where Wolf deftly caught it between his jaws.

"Good boy!" she said. Wolf growled.

Then she pulled out a chocolate bar.

"Excellent!" I said, reaching for it. She slapped my hand away.

"That's mine. This is for you." Jezebel handed me a brown paper package. Inside were some strips of dried beef, a wedge of cheese preserved in wax, and half a loaf of bread.

"Not bad," I said, surprised at how well she knew me.

"*Not bad?* That's all you can say after I snuck past Cook and pilfered half the icebox for you?" she asked, turning her nose up.

"Well, he did say 'excellent' until you slapped his hand and stole his chocolate," Wolf added helpfully.

"It was never his chocolate to begin with. Now that it's just us three, I can eat all the chocolate I want." With this, the countess sank her teeth into the candy and chewed with obvious delight.

We'd just finished our meal and were dusting the crumbs from our cloaks when—

"Rune!"

The voice made us all jump. I turned to see Chad materialize out of the woods with the Morgana kids.

He sounded surprised to see me, but I had the strangest feeling he'd been *trying* to run into us.

"Chad!" I said, also trying to sound surprised.

I couldn't let him know what I'd learned. At the moment, I had the advantage of secret knowledge. A villain always keeps his secrets secret. We learned that in Master Stiltskin's grandfather's autobiography, *If Only I'd Kept My Big Mouth Shut.*

You see, Rumpelstiltskin had nearly sealed the deal on taking a baby away from its mom—a favorite villain pastime. The one stipulation was if the mother could guess his name, Rumpel would let her keep the baby. This plan seemed foolproof until he blabbed his name out loud right in front of the mom's friend, who, being a gossipy busybody, told the mother. No baby for Rumpel . . . all because he couldn't just shut up.

"You must be Plotting," Chad said. "I didn't know you were allowed to bring anyone." He looked at Wolf and Jezebel.

"Uh, me either," I lied. "I just found out last night after you'd begun Plotting. Congratulations, by the way."

"Thanks," he said. Then he gestured to the Morgana kids. "Oh, you remember Erzsebet Bathory?" He indicated the vampire girl who'd been a jerk to us at Morgana's. Jez and I nodded while Wolf growled low and quiet. "And this is Gilles DeRay. Gilles, this is Rune Drexler, Countess Jezebel Dracula, and Wolf Junior." Chad pointed to each of us. The Morgana kids just sneered.

"Well, I'd invite you to lunch, but we've just finished and have a lot to do, so I guess we'll see you later?" I asked.

"Yes. Maybe we'll run into each other again," Chad said.

I bet we will. "Oh, sure. Can't wait." With a round of good-byes, Chad and his Conspirators melted into the darkness of the Forgotten Forest.

"Did you see that Erzsebet snob? I hope a giant squashes her ugly face into toe jam," Wolf Junior said.

"Let's get out of here. The sooner we're done with this Plot, the happier I'll be," Jez said.

"Not just yet, Jez. I have a feeling I know where Chad's going, and I'd like a little more information."

The time had come to try to use my dad's crystal ball.

The trouble with the crystal ball is it only shows what it wants. Sometimes that's okay. Sometimes not so much. For instance, a person can ask it, *Will I be rich and famous?* And it might show a picture of that person surrounded by beautiful mansions only for him to find out that he's just destined to become a real estate agent who *sells* mansions to famous people. Other times, it won't show anything at all.

I pulled it out of my pack and rubbed my hands over the smooth surface, willing it to show me Chad's destination.

Inside, the ball began to pulse with red light. A picture formed. I could see something long and wet and pink and—

"Wolf!"

A drop of slobber slipped from Wolf Junior's tongue and landed on the crystal ball, which instantly went dark. I turned to see Wolf looming over my shoulder, staring at the (now dark) crystal. I tried to get it to work again, but of course it wouldn't.

"Oops," he said.

"We'll have to do this the old-fashioned way. Wolf? Do you think you could track their scent for a while, maybe do a little spying?"

"Sure," he answered.

"Good. Jez and I will continue north. Don't let them see you. Just keep your eyes and ears—and nose—open."

"We should plan on a meeting place," Jez said.

"Right. Wolf, let's see the map," I said.

Wolf pulled out the map, but the only thing it showed along our chosen path was the village Jez had mentioned.

"It's called Ieri," I said, pronouncing it *eerie*.

"No, you pronounce it *yer*. Which means 'yesterday,'" Jez said.

"Thank you, Mistress Smartyfangs," I said.

This earned me a hiss and a slap to the back of my head from Jez.

"Let's just meet in the Ieri town square tomorrow evening," I said.

"What if something happens?" Wolf asked.

But he already knew the answer. If Wolf didn't show, we'd assume the worst and go on without him. It wasn't very nice, but we're villains. Not-very-nice is what we're all about.

After transferring some of the provisions to his pack, Wolf dropped on all fours, pressed his nose to the ground, and disappeared after Chad into the forest. Jez and I continued on the dark path north. Things didn't seem too bad. I mean, we knew Chad's whereabouts; we knew what he was up to—mostly. I was feeling pretty optimistic.

Then a light flared in the darkness, and I noticed some of the trees spontaneously combusting. I was just about to point this out to Jezebel, but she beat me to it.

"Dragon!" she yelled mere moments before turning into a bat with a *pop!*

So I was pretty much alone (except for the company of a frantic flying rodent) when a lizard the size of a house came bumbling out of the woods to my right. It had shimmering greenish scales, stubby wings that seemed stuck to its body somehow, flippers in front and clawed feet in back, followed by a long, spiked tail. All of this was topped by not one, not two, but three (yes, three!) dragon heads.

Smoke curled from the nostrils of its middle head,

which bared its fangs furiously. The head directly to the left of the middle had been singed a bit and seemed slightly dazed. However, the head to the right of the smoking middle head (let's call the middle head Smoky) was downright petrified. It ducked and darted trying to avoid Smoky's rage. I even thought I saw one of its eyes twitching. I could totally relate.

Jez landed on my shoulder and whispered in my ear, "It's just a kid. It still has the webbing pinning down its wings. But it must not be a baby because it looks like it's discovered how to blow fire. At least, that middle head has."

"Great, a dragon going through puberty!" I said.

Smoky seemed to be looking for an outlet for his dragon-sized teen angst, and then his red eyes fell on me. Cat-a-bats!

The other two heads—we'll call them Dazed and Twitchy—suddenly noticed that Smoky had found something to focus his anger on. All three heads were on a mission now to roast the kid and the flying rodent standing conveniently in the middle of the road.

"We are *so* going to be fried!" I said.

My final thought as the dragon trudged clumsily toward me was that I was going to die an unsung death, roasted by a giant, pubescent lizard. I would become a villain's cautionary tale. In dad's History of Villainy class, he would say, "Don't end up like Drexler! Always bring your SPF five million sunscreen while Plotting in the forest!"

"Jez," I said. "What's that spell we learned about deflecting dragon attacks? Something like:

"Hill and dale,
wing and scale,
my need is dire,
something, something fire—Cat-a-bats!"

Why did spells always have to rhyme? Why couldn't they just be simple, like *kill the dragon!* I was contemplating this when a figure tumbled out of the woods directly in front of me.

Its eyes darted frantically from left to right. It must have seen me and Jez and the fire-breathing lizard, but it took no notice as it ran toward the road. The creature had a dog's head and a body that looked like stone . . . almost like a gargoyle had broken off Notre Dame and decided to vacation in the evil enchanted forest. Even my fear of the dragon was put on hold as this seriously weird-looking creature ran in front of us and disappeared into the trees on the other side of the road.

"Where do you suppose that thing's running off to in such a hurry?" I asked.

"Uh, Rune," Jez said, nodding her little bat noggin toward the woods.

From the forest burst an enormous dragon. It descended upon the road in a fury and made the dragon in front of us look like a toy.

"We have to get out of here before this gets worse," Jez said.

"How could it possibly get worse?" I asked.

"How many heads are you counting on the big one?" Jez asked, ignoring my question.

I did a quick tally. "Twelve."

Five or six of the heads spotted (and immediately dismissed) me and poor, fluttering Jezebel.

"It doesn't seem to care about us," Jez said.

"Duh," I said. "We obviously aren't worth the trouble to something that huge! Eating us would be like eating a bread crumb—especially once all the heads have a bite!"

When the creature spotted the smaller dragon, it roared furiously, setting the surrounding trees ablaze.

"Time to go?" Jez asked.

"Oh, definitely."

We fled toward the woods. Behind us, Smoky huffed indignantly while Twitchy cowered. Poor Dazed was still, well, *dazed*. The immense dragon had no baby webbing to hold *its* wings down. It unleashed them with massive flapping motions, causing a mini cyclone that sent me and Jezebel tumbling backward.

It was bad enough for me, but poor Jez was blown around like a leaf. I reached up a hand to pluck her out of the air and scurried to the safety of the few trees that weren't ablaze. Together we watched as the big dragon roared and huffed at the littler dragon.

"I think that one is the parent," I said to Jezebel as I pointed at Papa D.

"Looks kinda mad," Jezebel said. "Reminds me of the way my dad looked during the cocoa incident."

"Well then, let's get out of here while it's distracted," I said.

Jez quickly agreed. She transformed back into a girl as we silently made our way deeper into the forest. Behind us Papa D. was using most of its heads to nudge Smoky and the gang off the road and back toward the forest. Smoky was still spewing thick tendrils of smoke from his nostrils, but without Twitchy or Dazed to back him up, he was pretty much defeated.

"Oh, by the way, thanks ever so much for abandoning me to a possible fiery death," I said.

"What do you mean?" Jez asked. "I stayed with you the whole time!"

"Yeah. A flying rat is *soooo* helpful!"

"Excuse me? Did you just call me a rat?" Jez asked as we dashed from tree to tree.

"Careful," I said. "We don't want to get lost in here."

"Don't try to change the subject, Rune!" Jez said.

"I'm not," I lied. "It's just we definitely don't want to run into that dog-headed thing . . . whatever it was. An ogre maybe?"

"Capcaun. It's called a capcaun," Jez said.

"Are they dangerous?" I asked. "I don't think I've ever seen one before."

"Oh, so now you want information from Mistress Smartyfangs."

I rolled my eyes. "Okay, okay, I'm sorry. Yes. Please inform me."

"Well, capcauns can be dangerous. Mostly they like to kidnap kids—specifically young ladies. They prefer princesses, or so the legends go."

"Really?" I asked, perking up. "I wish I'd known. I would've made him my henchman!"

"We were a little busy at the time, remember?" Jez asked.

CHAPTER SIX

Henchmen Don't Give Hugs

Oh, no. The sun's still up!"

Jez stepped out from the cave where we'd spent most of the day sleeping. Actually, it was where *she'd* spent the day sleeping. Somehow, I got stuck outside the cave "keeping an eye out for dragons."

We set out on foot again now that we'd had time to rest. Beams of sunlight pierced the dense forest canopy and stabbed at the ground like swords. Jezebel was in a bad temper because every few feet she risked stumbling into a patch of random sunlight. A slight sizzling sound alerted me to her predicament.

"Aaaa!" she screeched, quickly pulling up her hood. But it was too late.

A rosy red rash was blossoming on both her cheeks, not to mention her nose. The pink hue contrasted sharply with her ashy gray skin.

"Don't you think we should've found the road by now?" she asked, stepping carefully around another patch of sunlight.

We had planned on spending the night hidden in the forest, then returning to the road again in the morning. However, Jez was right. It was taking us a lot longer to find it than it should have. I was about to suggest we try a different direction when I heard something.

"What *is* that?" Jezebel asked.

We both squinted into the forest.

"I don't know," I answered. "I think it's coming from over there." I pointed toward a dense, overgrown hillock about thirty yards away.

"It sounds like some kind of animal chittering," Jez said.

"It sounds like giggling to me," I said.

Suddenly, there was a deep moan followed by a thunderous splash, then more chitter-giggles. Jez and I exchanged nervous glances and moved forward cautiously.

"This is the part in the stories where trouble starts for the hero," I said.

"Good thing we're not heroes." Jez shot me a look. I couldn't argue with that kind of logic.

As we got closer to the hillock, I could make out the sounds more clearly. I heard a stream or small waterfall of some kind. There was definitely someone or some*thing* moaning as if in pain. The chittering animal sounds were more distinct too.

Jezebel and I crept silently to the edge of the hillock and peered over. Beneath us a scene unfolded. A stream wound and bubbled around the base of the hillock. About twenty feet below us, it formed a deep, glittering pool before moving on around the hill and out of sight.

Gathered around the pool were about a dozen little critters, each no bigger than my hand.

"Sprites!" I whispered.

No two looked alike, and yet they all shared similar features. Some wore pointy hats made of acorns; others wore curling shoes adorned with tiny charms and bells. One was as thin as a string bean, another fat and stumpy. Yet all of them seemed as though they were formed from bits and pieces of the forest combined with mix-and-match animal parts like tusks or horns. The little sprites also had hands and feet, which made them look a little like people too. We watched as some of the tiny sprites hopped and skipped in a circle while turning a wooden crank attached to a rope.

"What is that thing?" Jez asked, pointing at a much larger being dangling upside down from the rope.

"It's one of those ogre creatures!" I said excitedly.

"Capcaun," Jez corrected.

The beast's skin was the color of rocks—gray and flecked. He wore only a pair of cut-off pants that might have been blue once, but had become faded and frayed. His doglike head hung just a few feet above the water. As we watched, the ogre whimpered in agony, anticipating what would happen next.

Sure enough, the little creatures who had been cranking the rope stopped and, all at once, let go. There was a moment of complete silence. The sprites all stopped moving and chittering to watch the poor dog-headed ogre plunge headfirst into the pool. As soon as his head hit the water, the sprites erupted in fits of laughter. Then they hoisted the beast up and did it all over again.

"We should get back to the road," Jezebel said. She didn't seem to particularly care about the sprites or their captive, but I did.

"No way," I said. "We have to capture that ogre to be my henchman!"

"Are you serious?" Jezebel asked. "What could a capcaun do that you can't?"

"Capture a princess. You said yourself that's what they do."

"In *legends*, Rune," said Jez. "In real life they probably whine and slobber and eat all your chocolate."

"You are downright stingy with chocolate. Besides,

I have to find a henchman! It's part of the Plot. And it won't even be hard to capture him. Look. The sprites have already done the work for us." I pointed at the scene below as evidence.

Jez sighed dramatically, then itched at her nose where the blotchy red rash was finally fading a little.

"So, what's the plan?" she asked. I knew she'd come around.

"We'll just go tell them we want their ogre," I said.

She looked at me like I was crazy. Why do girls always think a perfectly simple plan (like demanding the release of a prisoner from unstable magical creatures) is crazy?

"And you think they'll just hand him right over?"

"Sure. Why not?" I asked.

Jez rolled her eyes as I gave her my most roguish smile. Then we made our way down the hill. The sprites had just hauled the ogre up for another dunking when one of them spotted us. I couldn't tell what he was saying, because I don't speak sprite gibberish, but the frantic jumping and pointing kind of tipped me off. Soon, all the sprites had gathered around us, except for a handful who struggled at the crank, trying to hold the capcaun up in the air.

One of the sprites approached us and began gesturing rudely. He must've been their leader, because his toes were longer and curlier than the rest; plus he wore a bright jewel on a makeshift crown made of woven sticks. (Closer inspection revealed the jewel to be just an ordinary drop of water trapped within the crown.) He prattled on and on in his twittering voice.

"Look," I said. "I have no clue what you're saying, but we need your ogre—"

"Capcaun," Jez corrected.

"*Capcaun*, so hand him over and nobody gets squished."

"Smooth," Jez muttered. I ignored her.

The tiny sprite didn't seem to understand. I tried miming. First, I pointed at the ogre. Then I pointed at the sprite leader. Then I took my fist and pounded it onto my palm in a way I hoped was threatening.

Apparently, some part of my message got through, because as soon as I'd finished, the sprites began running around in a panicky sort of way.

There was another loud splash. With no one to man the crank, the ogre had fallen once more into the water. The little sprites scattered like roaches, disappearing into the forest.

"Give me a hand," I said to Jez as I ran over to the creature and untied his leg.

"Ewww. No way. I'll get *wet*."

"How is it girls can spend three hours soaking in a

hot bath but can't manage a few drips from a sopping ogre?" I asked.

"Capcaun," Jez said. "And you're really going to accuse *me* of too much tub time? I seem to recall last week a line stretching from the bath caves to the Great Clock and several students complaining that Rune Drexler was in the tub again taking his sweet time—"

"Let's not dredge up the past," I said quickly.

I managed to untie the creature on my own. At this point I was expecting him to attempt escape, so I held out my arms, ready to grab him the minute he stood up. This was a bad idea for two reasons.

First, the ogre had no intention of escape, so my attempts to capture him were pointless. Second—and this was really the clincher—he mistook my open arms for an invitation to *hug* me. He raised his dripping wet, stony body out of the pool and embraced me in a great big bear hug that nearly crushed my ribs.

"Ewww!" I said as he soaked my clothes.

"What's wrong, Rune?" Jez asked with a smirk. "Can't manage a few drips from a sopping ogre?"

"Capcaun," I said irritably.

"Little man save Cappy. Best friends!" the creature said in a deep, slow voice. I started to rethink my plan to make him my henchman—especially when Jezebel erupted in giggles.

"Good job capturing a henchman, Rune. Now I think the trick will be getting rid of him," she said between fits of laughter.

I pushed the capcaun away from me. He stumbled back to the water's edge, where he just stood like a stone statue, his arms dangling like a gorilla's as he stared at me with clueless gratitude.

"Look here," I said, trying to sound authoritative. "What do you know about kidnapping princesses?"

He stared at me for a full thirty seconds. When a thin string of drool began to dangle from the corner of his slack jaw, I decided he wasn't going to answer me. Time to elaborate.

"Princesses? Hello?" I snapped my fingers in front of his face. He smiled and nodded. Not a good sign.

"Purdy girly," he said, eyeing Jezebel, who suddenly stopped laughing.

"Hey!" she said in alarm as the capcaun lumbered toward her. "Stop! Don't come near me. I mean it!"

The capcaun completely ignored Jezebel's warning. I worried he didn't realize who he was dealing with. Sure, Jez was just a halfsie, but her bite could be as lethal as a full-fledged vampire's. She backed away, baring her teeth, but the brainless creature grabbed her arm.

"No, Jez! Don't!" I shouted. Too late.

Before I could stop her, Jezebel sank her fangs into his clawed hand.

"Yow!" he and Jez both cried simultaneously.

The capcaun pulled his hand away and stuck out his bottom lip like a two-year-old. There was a small scratch where Jez had bitten, but the skin remained unbroken. Jezebel raised her fingers to her mouth.

"I think he nearly chipped my tooth!" she cried, wiggling each of her teeth experimentally.

"He must be immune to vampires," I said thoughtfully. Maybe he had some magical properties after all—or maybe he really was made of stone.

"Mean bitey girly!" The capcaun pouted, frowning at Jezebel.

"Mean grabby gargoyle!" Jezebel retaliated.

"Good one, Jez," I said sarcastically. She hissed at me.

"Okay, I think we got off on the wrong foot here. My name is Rune. What's your name?" I asked.

"Name Cappy."

"Cappy. Nice to meet you. This is Jezebel." I pointed to Jez, who glared at the capcaun. He eyed her with obvious and open mistrust.

"Okay, introductions over. Listen, Cappy, did you like those mean sprites tying you up and dunking you in the river?" I thought it would be best to remind him we had just saved him.

"No! Spriteys mean. Cappy no like wet," he said, scratching behind one of his gray dog ears with his clawed fingers.

"And aren't you glad we rescued you?" I asked, trying to drop a hint.

"Cappy *glaaaaaad*," he said, smiling at me. He had two enormous bottom teeth that curved up over his doglike snout when he smiled. It was funny and a little frightening. I could see why Jez bit him.

"Right, glad. Good. So, wouldn't you like to help *us* now, Cappy?"

"Cappy help!" he answered, smiling even bigger. "Cappy help *Ruuuuney*."

"Swell. So, would you like to be my henchman?"

Another thirty seconds passed as Cappy smiled stupidly. Smaller words. I had to use smaller words.

"Would you like to help us find a pretty girly?" I asked.

"Pretty! Pretty girly!" He smiled and jumped, shaking the ground. "No meany girlies with pointy teethies!" he said, frowning at Jezebel again.

She hissed at him.

"Cut it out, Jez," I said.

"I don't want him coming with us!" she said.

I pulled her aside.

"Look, we don't have many options here. Let's

take him along. If we find something better, we'll dump him. Agreed?"

Jez looked over my shoulder at the dripping ogre.

"Fine," she said.

"Girly mad?" Cappy asked, his eyes huge and sad. I think he already forgot Jez had bitten him.

There was a long pause. Finally, I elbowed Jez. She sighed dramatically.

"No, Cappy. I'm not mad."

"There, see? All is forgiven. Nice girly." I smiled, patting Jez on the head. She pinched my arm.

"Ow!" I said, pulling away. "Okay, Cappy, if you're going to be my henchman, you need to know one very important rule: henchmen don't give hugs. Got that? Good. Now, come with us."

But he really didn't have a choice because at that moment, a rainstorm of miniature arrows arced out from behind the trees and stabbed at me and Jez like a hundred stinging needles. Cappy seemed immune. His hard, rocklike skin deflected the barrage. Still, he appeared kind of angry all the same.

From behind tree trunks and leaves, little black eyes glared at us. The sprites had returned with reinforcements. I guess I hadn't scared them off after all. Jez turned into a bat and flew away.

"Girly can *fly*," Cappy said in awe.

"Yeah, ouch! Super," I replied, pulling my cloak over my head to deflect the tiny arrows. "Way to stick together, Jez! C'mon Cappy! Let's—ouch!—get out of here."

I ran in the direction Jez had flown.

Cappy lumbered after me, kicking sprites left and right with his big clawed feet. They sailed through the air, landed hard on their rumps, and chattered angrily, shaking their fists at us. It was a relief to make it back into the protection of the surrounding trees.

Cappy and I ran on for a few more minutes until we finally caught up with Jezebel. I was glad to see we hadn't lost her; however, we *had* lost something. The road. Now I *really* had no idea which direction it was in.

"Jez, why don't you fly up and have a look around? At least you can be *some* use to us as a bat."

"Hey! I can't help it, okay? When I get nervous I just, just . . ."

"Abandon people?"

"No!" she shouted. "Oh, forget it!"

She flew up above the forest, but even from above, the trees crowded in so close that Jezebel couldn't see the road anywhere.

The afternoon had turned to evening. The forest deepened to a cool, velvety purple. The second day of my Plot was quickly slipping away, and now I'd lost the road. We decided to stop for a bite to eat before moving on. Cappy found a dead rabbit and was munching it—fur, bones, and all. Jezebel and I ate from the provisions she'd packed. I think she could tell I was a little depressed, because she offered me a bite of her chocolate.

We got a fire going, then Jez and I took turns pulling out sprite arrows from each other's skin like splinters.

"Are you still mad?" she asked as she plucked one from my neck.

"Ouch! Mad? About what?" I asked.

"I don't mean to, you know, transform all the time. It just . . . happens. When I get anxious."

"Oh."

Fighting with Jez was fun, but for some reason talking seriously to her made *me* anxious.

"I'm not mad. I just can't believe we lost the road. If only we had some way to—wait a minute!"

I rummaged in my pack and pulled out my dad's crystal ball. Jez scooted in for a closer look. Our hands touched the glassy surface at the same time. I expected her to shy away, maybe flutter her eyelashes at me, but who was I kidding? This was Jez. After a tiny moment of awkwardness, she slapped my hand and took the crystal ball from me.

"Let me do it this time," she said, closing her eyes and running her hands over the sleek surface. "Show us the road."

A moment later, a familiar red glow lit up the ball. Cappy even stopped munching his rabbit to watch. His eyes got all big like he was being hypnotized.

"Ooooh, purdy!"

An image formed inside the ball of a dark road surrounded by trees.

"Well, that's really helpful," I said. "Nice work, Jez. It showed us the road all right. Now if we only knew HOW TO GET THERE!"

The crystal went stubbornly dark.

"Oh, like you could do any better! Anyway, don't be such a baby. We'll find the road again. There's no way I'm going to tell my dad I failed my first Plot," she said.

"Me neither," I said.

Cappy was no help at all. He had no idea where anything was.

"But you live here!" I said to him, exasperated.

Cappy just smiled stupidly until a moth flew past. He hopped up and down, chasing it around the forest. But when he finally caught it, he smashed it in his clumsy, clawed hands. He cried for almost an hour.

"Poor flutterby!" he moaned from a rock, where he sat with his dog head in his claws.

"I wonder how Wolf Junior is doing," I said to Jez.

"Doggy?" Cappy asked, perking with interest.

"Yeah, Cappy. He's a doggy. You'll get to meet Wolf later, okay? If we ever get out of here. We're lost, Jez."

"I know," she answered. "But there has to be some way . . ."

"There isn't!" I yelled.

Cappy's bawling and Jez's unrelenting determination were getting on my nerves. I only had five days left to steal a baby, kidnap a princess, and overthrow a kingdom . . . and I was stuck in the forest with an optimistic vampire and a crybaby henchman.

I'd pretty much given up hope, when something strange happened.

"Did you hear that?" Jez said. Even Cappy stopped crying to listen.

"It sounded like Wolf. Maybe we're not lost!" I said. "Wolf! Where are you?"

From far away we heard the voice again shouting what might have been our names.

"He's calling us!" Jez said. "Wolf! Over here!"

Quickly, Jez became a bat and flew in the direction of the voice. I put out our fire—except for one branch, which I used as a torch—and ran after her. Cappy trudged behind.

For a moment, I thought we'd lost track of Wolf's voice. Then we heard it again a little farther away. Once again, we ran after it only to come up empty.

"Where did he go?" I asked, searching around frantically.

All I could see were trees and thick undergrowth

in all directions. Then I heard the voice again. This time, Wolf was calling from our left. I ran toward the sound, shouting Wolf's name. Instead of getting closer, though, the voice stayed just beyond our reach.

Jez had transformed back into a girl and Cappy had finally caught up with us, when we all stumbled through a thick growth of brambles and straight into what seemed like an enormous patch of soft moss. The moonlight broke through the canopy and turned the moss into an eerie misty green.

"Ooooh," Cappy said. "Pretty greeny."

We stepped into the mossy clearing just as a hailstorm of tiny arrows rained down on us from all directions. I tried to duck behind Cappy and realized I couldn't move my feet.

"Cappy stuck!" the capcaun cried anxiously.

"I'm stuck too!" Jez said in alarm. "And I can't transform!"

My feet sank beneath the surface of the moss, and I realized what had happened. Somehow the sprites had imitated Wolf's voice and lured us into a trap.

"Rune! What do we do?" Jez asked, trying to pull her legs free. She only sank faster.

"Stop struggling! It's a Magic Marsh!" I said. "We have to think." A Magic Marsh is like quicksand, only it keeps a person from using magic to escape.

The barrage of mini arrows stopped as the little sprite

chief stepped into the moonlight with his followers. He pointed at me, then Jez, then Cappy. Then he made a fist and pounded it into his other hand.

"Yeah, I get it," I said irritably to the little sprite. He pointed and laughed. The others all joined in.

"Jerks!" I yelled.

Villains were not supposed to fall into lame traps. They were supposed to *make* the traps. Wolf Junior's dad is the expert on this subject. He wrote *Grandma's House: What I'd Do Differently* after the whole Red Riding Hood debacle.

I tried desperately to think of a plan as we sank deeper and deeper into the Magic Marsh. The marsh quickly swallowed us up to our waists, and every few seconds, one of the sprites would release an arrow at us just for fun. One stuck in Jez's nose, which really ticked her off. She hissed and tried to grab the sprites, but they remained just out of reach.

A moment later, an enormous bubble erupted from beneath the surface of the marsh. Green moss arced upward as the stinking air escaped.

"Gross, Cappy," I said. He looked at me for a moment, uncomprehending.

"Cappy no toot," he said finally. I raised my eyebrow at Jez.

"It wasn't me!" she huffed.

Suddenly, we started sinking ten times faster than before. My makeshift torch went out. In no time, we were up to our shoulders in foul, mucky marsh.

"Oh, no!" Jez yelled.

"It must've been an air pocket holding us up," I said.

I racked my brain to think of a way to save us, but I couldn't come up with anything.

On the shore, the little chieftain and his gang stopped their twittering laughter. They all crossed their arms over their chests and narrowed their eyes at us. Then a slow, malicious smirk spread across the chief's face. They weren't just playing. We were doomed.

"Rune, what do we do?" Jezebel asked. I could hear the fear in her voice.

"I don't know," I said.

"Rune," Jez said after a moment.

"Yeah?"

"If this is really the end, then I just want to tell you— Hey!"

Out of the woods, a blinding light flashed. I squinted, and when my vision cleared I saw three beautiful flying creatures. They weren't much bigger than the sprites, but they couldn't have looked more different. Where the sprites seemed earthy and crude, the flying ladies were creatures of the air, lovely and refined—like royalty.

"Help!" I shouted to them. It was our last hope.

At the sight of the beautiful fairylike women, the sprites fell on their faces and groveled. The lady in front held a little stick that glowed at the tip. She reminded me of a white rose. As she raised her magic wand, the sprite chieftain floated up into the air in front of her.

"Gobledeegrigglebee?" she said to him in sprite-gibberish.

He nodded. Then she pointed at us, and he nodded again. Finally, she shook her head at him as if she were very disappointed. He burst into tears.

"Oh, Tibix!" one of the flying ladies said.

"What have you done now?" asked another.

The fairies flew in a little circle around the floating sprite chieftain and continued to interrogate him in the weird gibberish-talk.

All this I watched in silence. I couldn't speak if I wanted to, because my lips had just sunk beneath the mossy surface of the Magic Marsh. My eyes darted to Jez and Cappy, who weren't faring much better. Jez's nose was just dipping into the moss while Cappy had tilted his head back so that his face seemed to be resting on the lake like a floating dinner plate.

This was it. I was going to die. And what was worse . . . I was going to die without completing my Plot. Some people might think I had my priorities a little backward, but if they'd been trained as a villain from the time they were two years old, they would've felt exactly the same.

I contemplated the look on Chad's freckled, bespectacled face when he found out I'd been beaten by a bunch of three-inch-tall pixies. I sucked a desperate last breath into my nostrils before my head sank under.

CHAPTER SEVEN

Grand Theft Baby

I'd been under precisely twelve seconds when my head miraculously emerged from the marsh. At first I thought another bubble had risen up to carry me to the surface for one final, taunting breath before plunging me back under the muck. But I didn't go back under. I rose up and up and up. I stared wide eyed at Jez and Cappy, who were also rising out of the marsh. In seconds, we were floating over the surface and onto solid ground.

"We're alive!" Jez said, throwing her soggy arms around me. I smiled with relief.

"Hey, what were you saying before?" I asked.

"Uh . . . ," Jez said, quickly pulling away and pointing.

I looked up to find the three glowing ladies smiling at us. Better yet, the sprite chief was *bowing* to us. He had taken off his crown and held it to his chest like a hat. Then he said something in gibberish, which the glowing white rose lady translated.

"Tibix apologizes for waylaying you and your friends," she said. Her voice sounded like three-part harmony. At first, I thought the other ladies were speaking too, but their mouths didn't move.

"Uh, thanks. I guess," I said to the little chief.

I could tell *Tibix* would've preferred to let us drown. When he thought the flying lady wasn't looking, he stuck his tongue out at me. Then he yelped as she zapped him with her wand.

"Quit that," she said sternly to the little chieftain. "You may go, Tibix."

The chieftain didn't need to be told twice. In the time it took me to blink, Tibix and his sprites had melted into the darkling forest. Jez, Cappy, and I were left alone with the three glowing ladies.

Now that I wasn't about to die, I had time to study their features. The white rose lady's hair was long and white, but her face was both young and wise. She wore white petals around her waist that flowed into a gown. On her head was a crown.

The other two fairylike women resembled her, but the one to the right had golden hair and reminded me of a dandelion or maybe a daisy. As a villain I don't really know that much about flowers.

The lady on the left had dark skin, coppery hair, and a bright orange dress. I think it was made from a poppy. (Okay, I definitely knew too much about flowers. I made a mental note never to mention this knowledge out loud. It would completely ruin my villainous reputation.)

"Come with us," the white rose lady said in her harmonic voice. "We'll find you shelter, clothes, whatever you need, children."

All seemed well until Cappy wiped the muck from his dog face. The flying ladies took one look at him and flew backward, frowning at us.

"Not that one, sister!" the daisy lady said.

"He's a capcaun!" the poppy lady added.

The white rose lady seemed to scrutinize us very closely. I sensed that if she found out we were villains, we might be in trouble. I hoped Jez would keep her teeth hidden and refrain from turning into a bat. Our lives might depend on it.

"He's with us!" I said. "His name is Cappy. He's very gentle. Really. He was . . . uh . . . helping us get to the village of Ieri."

"He is your guide?" the rose lady asked. I could tell she wasn't buying it.

"Sort of," I answered. "We found him being tortured by those sprite creatures, and we saved him.

He's trying to repay the favor." This was almost true.

"Pretty flutterbies!" Cappy said, smiling at the flying ladies. He stepped forward as if to grab one of them, but I held him back with one hand and whispered, "Not now, Cappy."

The flying ladies took a moment to confer as they hovered in the air. Then the white rose lady said, "We will take you to the village. We have business there this night. Follow us."

I couldn't believe our luck. We fell in line behind the ladies, who illuminated the forest in front of us with their soft glow. Under my breath I asked Jezebel, "Are they fairies?"

"Pretty much. They're called the Zâne," she whispered. "They're known for bestowing gifts on the good . . . especially children. They sometimes bless babies with unique powers. But they also punish evil, sometimes severely, so watch your step. That's why they didn't like Cappy."

"He's not evil," I said (rather regretfully, actually).

"He's an exception to the rule, Rune. Most capcauns are known for being destructive and malevolent."

At that moment, Cappy was picking his big doggy nose. Well, there are always exceptions to the rule, I guess. Who was I to judge? I mean, after all, most of the villains at Master Dreadthorn's School for Wayward Villains had, at some point, behaved in very un-villain-ish ways—like vampires drinking cocoa and big bad wolves rescuing drowning kids.

"Wait," I whispered. "You said they bless babies?"

"Yeah, why? Oh!" Jez said, comprehending.

"Let's keep our eyes open. For now, we'll just play the part of the poor lost kids."

I smiled as Jez batted her eyes innocently. She was pretty good at playing a poor lost kid.

The Zâne led us to a series of caves where we were each taken aside by one of the three fairies. The poppy took Jezebel down one of the caves while I followed the white rose lady. The daisy got stuck with Cappy, but she didn't seem to mind. She smiled and flew around his head saying, "Follow the pretty flutterby, Cappy!" He lumbered after her, laughing deeply.

I followed the rose fairy down a cave tunnel and into a dazzling grotto. Ivy and vines clung to the walls, reaching up toward the moonlit surface of the forest floor. For a split second, I thought I saw a flash of green in the willow strands, but when I blinked it was gone. I decided it must've been a shimmer of moonlight.

Below, the cave floor opened into a deep pool of water. I would've said it was the most beautiful place I'd ever seen . . . but villains don't say things like that.

"Here is one of our sacred pools," the rose fairy said. "You may bathe and rest. When you are clean, you may wrap yourself in the lambs' leaves while we wash your garments."

She pointed to a plant growing near the edge of the pool. Its leaves were bigger than my whole body. I didn't particularly relish the idea of wearing nothing but leaves, but I didn't really have a choice, since my clothes were a stinking, wet, mucky mess. The rose lady left me alone to bathe.

In minutes, I'd submerged myself in the warm water, allowing my worries to wash away with the grime. As a general rule, villains do *not* enjoy steamy, scented baths in beautiful fairy grottos. However, I was willing to let it slide—this time.

At some point, the rose fairy must have come back for my clothes, because when I came out of my reverie, they were gone. I floated over to the gigantic lambs' leaves and reached out to pluck one. They were incredibly soft. In a few moments, I'd covered myself with the lambs' leaf, using it as a makeshift towel. I was really starting to worry about how un-villainlike I must look at the moment, but I assured myself this was all part of the plan. We had to look like innocent kids if we wanted the Zâne's help, right?

I made my way back out of the cave and into a

clearing where Cappy waited with the fairy ladies. A split second later, Jez emerged also wearing a lambs' leaf towel.

"Whoa," I said. Usually Jez was head-to-toe black with a cloak over it all.

"Aren't these *sooooo* soft?" she asked, twirling like she was wearing a new dress or something.

"Uh-huh," I said, trying to look anywhere but at Jez and her skimpy veggie-towel. This resulted in me stubbing my toe, tripping over a rock, and walking face-first into a tree.

"Walk much?" Jez asked, tossing her hair over her shoulder and gliding past me.

Girls.

We sat next to a fire that flickered with strange blue flames. The Zâne brought us bowls of berries and apples. Cappy and Jez began munching happily.

"Your clothing is already nearly dry," the rose lady said. I could see our cloaks (and Cappy's cut-offs) hanging on a tree branch near the fire. "When you've eaten and rested, we will guide you to the village."

"Thank you," I said. (What? Villains can't have manners?)

I joined Jezebel and Cappy. In a few minutes, we had finished the fruit and were dozing near the fire. It seemed I'd only closed my eyes for a moment when the rose fairy was shaking me.

"Midnight approaches. Wake up, child," she said.

"Just a few more minutes," I whined, rolling over.

"I'm afraid not. The time draws near when our presence is needed in the village."

I roused myself from sleep, wondering what kind of business the three fairies would have in Ieri. Could they be blessing a baby? Could I possibly get *that* lucky? I didn't dare to hope, but secretly began to calculate what I would do if we found a baby there.

Soon, Jez, Cappy, and I were clothed once more and following the Zâne through the forest. It was hard to tell how much time had gone by; aside from the glow of the Zâne, the forest was as black as Master Dreadthorn's onyx desk. Thinking of the desk made me think of the crystal ball. Thinking of the ball made me think of Chad, and thinking of Chad made me worry. What if he was the one who'd sent the sprites after us? Or maybe the Zâne were under his command. Maybe they were leading us to Muma Padurii's gingerbread house.

But I had nothing to fear. In less than thirty minutes, we entered a clearing that turned out to be the road. Overhead, shredded clouds ghosted across the moon.

It was nearing two o'clock in the morning when I noticed another light.

"Do you see that?" Jez asked. "I think it's the village."

It started as only a mild glow far ahead of us. Then I realized the trees were getting smaller and fewer. We were coming out of the Forgotten Forest.

"Finally," I said, relieved that the forest—and its numerous deathtraps—would soon be left behind.

We emerged completely from the shadows of the trees and into open land just as a light rain began. The hill we were standing on sloped gently downward, into a valley. The village of Ieri was just below us at the foot of the hill twinkling with firelight.

I turned around to see the Forgotten Forest looming behind us. For a moment, I was sure I saw a small shadow move in the trees. Could Chad have sent someone—or something—to spy on me? No, I was being paranoid; it was probably just an owl or something.

"Our magic will not last long outside of the forest," the white rose lady said. "We can only stay in the village as long as darkness lasts."

"That's okay," I said. "We can take it from here."

"Oh?" she asked. "And what are your plans for Cappy? He will surely be shunned by the villagers. I fear for your safety. Perhaps he should remain in the forest?"

"No!" I said, a little more severely than I meant. "I mean, we've grown . . . uh . . . fond of Cappy—right, Jez?" I jabbed Jezebel with my elbow.

"Huh? Oh! Yes, very fond of him and . . . uh . . . he doesn't have any friends or family in the forest anyway," Jez said. I had no idea if this was true, but Cappy didn't argue. He just smiled his big, dumb smile.

"And we have a friend we're meeting in the village square," I added.

"Then perhaps we can accompany you until the time for our departure arrives?" the white rose fairy said.

I couldn't think of a good argument. I especially didn't want to insult the Zâne's hospitality after all the help they'd given us. But what would happen when they saw we were meeting Wolf in the village? Surely they'd know we were villains, and then what?

We didn't have a choice. The Zâne were already leading the way down the rain-soaked hill into the village. Jez, Cappy, and I followed behind them.

When we neared the town, we could see it had an enormous wall built all around it. The gates had been shut for the night, and beyond the gate we could hear the sound of guards playing a dice game.

"Now what?" Jez asked as we stood shivering in the wet cold. "That wall must be thirty feet high!"

Jez and I exchanged glances, and I knew what she was thinking. If the fairies had just stayed behind in the forest, Jez could transform into a bat and fly over, unlocking the gate from within. But as it turned out, she didn't have to.

"I think we can manage," the poppy fairy said.

She flew over the gate toward the guardhouse and disappeared. In a matter of minutes, she returned announcing the coast was clear. We pushed through the now unlocked gate and found the guards sleeping soundly in the guardhouse with their arms crossed over their chests and big smiles on their faces.

We made our way to the village square without any trouble. It seemed the entire village was asleep, and anyone who did happen to be up late suddenly got very sleepy as we approached, and they rushed into their houses, closing their doors and turning off their lights.

The village square was lit all around by torches. They had burned low in the rain but still gave off a faint glow. In the middle of the square was a well—the main water supply for the village. I knew in the morning it would be crowded with townspeople, but for now the place was deserted. I expected to find Wolf sitting there, waiting for us, but he wasn't.

I remembered the Zâne had said Cappy might not be welcomed in the village because of what he was. I thought maybe Wolf had had the same idea. Perhaps he had been hiding nearby waiting for us to show up. We made our way to the well and waited. And waited. And waited. No Wolf. Finally, the Zâne grew restless.

"Perhaps your friend mistook the time?" the daisy lady said.

"Maybe," I answered, exchanging a look with Jezebel.

"I'm afraid we can't wait with you much longer," said the white rose lady. "We have urgent business, and I sense the time is near at hand."

"Um, if you don't mind my asking . . . what exactly *is* your business here in town tonight?" Jez asked. It was the question I had wanted to ask but was too chicken . . . I mean, too *cautious* to ask myself.

"You will soon see. Look! Someone approaches!" the poppy lady said, pointing to a dark alley on the opposite side of the square.

"Come with us. Quickly!" said the white rose lady.

We followed the Zâne into the shadowy overhang of a tailor's shop and watched as a figure emerged from the alley. At first, I thought it might be Wolf, but I quickly ruled that out. The figure was too slender beneath the hooded cloak. A woman, then. She clutched tightly to something as she flitted like a wraith from shadow to shadow.

"What's she doing?" Jezebel whispered.

"Watch and see," the daisy fairy said sadly.

The woman dashed into the open space of the town square and stopped at the well. She lifted her hood to reveal a very young, lovely face, although it was twisted with worry. Then she uncovered the bundle she'd been holding so tightly. From our position across the square, it was impossible to see what she had uncovered. And yet, somehow, I knew. The gentle way she pulled the blanket. The soft kiss as she dusted its face with her cheek. It was a baby.

Jez and I both exchanged excited looks.

Jackpot! I mouthed to Jez, making sure the fairies weren't watching us.

The woman bent over the well and with mounting horror I thought she would drop the baby into the deep water. And I couldn't care less about the baby's *safety*. That's just cracked! I was only worried about losing a chance to steal the kid—I was pretty sure it needed to be a *live* one.

But I had nothing to fear. The woman laid the baby gently on the rain-soaked grass near the well. She tucked a note carefully into the folds of the blanket. Then, with one final glance behind her, she pulled the cloak hood over her head and melted into the shadows.

In a matter of moments, we had all crossed the square to where the sleeping baby lay. Even in the dark, I could see tufts of bright red curls peeking out from under the blanket's frayed edge.

Now I just had to figure out how to convince the Zâne to let me have the stinky little thing. My planning was interrupted by an outburst from Jez.

"Why did she do that?" she said. I was shocked at the accusation in her voice. "How could anybody do that!"

"Shh. Be still, child," the white rose lady said. "It will be for the best. You'll see."

Jezebel plucked the note from the blanket, being careful not to wake the sleeping infant.

"What's it say?" I asked as we stood in the rain, which was fading into a misty drizzle.

"It says she was a poor girl who could not afford to take care of her precious baby. It says 'Please love her as I always will.'"

Jez wiped quickly at her eyes and sniffled. I'd never thought of the countess as the kind of girl to get all choked up over an abandoned baby. She noticed me watching her.

"What? I'm probably just getting a dumb cold from all this rain," she said.

However, Jez's reaction was not the biggest surprise. That award went to Cappy. One look at the little pink bundle and he was hooked.

"Oooooh," he said, grabbing for the baby with his big, clumsy claws. I reached out to stop him, but the Zâne held me back.

"Just a moment," the white rose lady said, smiling affectionately at Cappy and the baby. It seemed all the Zâne had changed their minds about him. You might even say they'd grown fond of him.

Cappy scooped the bundled baby into his massive ape-arms with a surprising gentleness I would not have thought possible from the big oaf—especially after he'd pulverized that moth. He cradled the baby close to his chest as if he'd done it a thousand times before.

"Hold her close, Cappy, while we bless her," the white rose lady said.

Then the Zâne gathered around the baby's head, floating in a slow, revolving circle as they extended their hands over her—the white rose lady holding her magic wand. They whispered in a language I had never heard, and yet it sounded familiar. It was the sound of wind in the trees and clear, cool streams bubbling over rocks. It was the sound of the moon and the stars and *cat-a-bats!* Those girly fairy spells were making me all crazy and mushy. Thankfully, they stopped singing before I ended up in a cape fighting for justice and honor and junk like that.

Each of the Zâne touched the baby's soft forehead with their tiny hands. Then it was over.

"That's it?" I asked. "I mean . . . what now?"

"That is for you to decide, Rune," the white rose lady said. "This baby's fate is tied up with yours now. In time, you will see her gifts. She is a very special baby."

"Wait . . . you mean, we're supposed to take it, uh, *her* with us?" I asked. This baby stealing was a piece of cake!

"That is also for you to decide. However, even if you were to leave her here by this well, it is our belief that she would somehow find a way to reach you. As I said, your fates are intertwined now."

"Pretty baby. Pretty baby sleepy," Cappy whispered as he rocked the baby tenderly.

"And now, dawn is approaching. The moon sets. We must be away," the poppy lady said. I couldn't see any hint of morning light, but I wasn't going to argue.

"Oh, uh, thanks for all your help," I said. "We'll take, uh, good care of it . . . I mean *her*."

Then the Zâne were gone in a flash of light, and we were alone in the middle of the town with a baby and no Wolf.

"Score!" I shouted. "That was *easy!*"

At that moment, the baby woke up and started to cry.

"What now?" Jezebel asked, wrinkling her nose. It seemed her previous concern did not extend to *crying* babies.

"Ummm . . . ," I said. "We need a goat."

"Are you mental?" Jez started counting on her fingers. "Henchman, baby, princess, kingdom. I don't remember 'goat' anywhere in the Plot, Rune."

"Milk, Countess Know-It-All. The quickest way to shut a kid up is to feed it."

After a hasty search, we found a goat at the other

end of town, tethered to a fencepost. We untied it and led it a few feet down the road when I thought better of it and went back to leave one of my gold coins on the fencepost.

"What are you doing?" Jez asked.

"I can't have the whole town chasing us with pitchforks and torches looking for the village goat, now, can I?"

Jez just rolled her eyes.

We decided that we couldn't wait for Wolf. We had to keep moving. With dawn on the horizon, the town of Ieri would soon be awake and wondering what a dog-headed monster was doing with a redheaded baby and what a couple of villains were doing with a pilfered goat. So we crossed over the border into the kingdom of Kaloya.

CHAPTER EIGHT

On the Road Again

Are there always this many patrols?" Jez asked.

"I don't know," I answered.

We'd slept most of the day in a grove of trees about thirty yards from the road, waking in a late, cloudy afternoon. From the shadows of our hiding spot, we watched as yet another patrol of soldiers went by. The roads were crawling with them. We were forced to keep to the trees and fields, so we wouldn't be questioned. Jez and I might have been able to explain why we were traveling with a baby and no guardians, but there was no way we could explain Cappy.

"I wish we had some means of knowing what was going on," Jez said.

"Oh, duh!" I answered. "We do!" I reached into my pack and found my dad's crystal ball.

I rubbed my hands over the smooth, glassy surface until the ball started to glow. In it I saw a city. Kaloya was in turmoil over a recent uprising at the palace. Soldiers were being dispatched to patrol all major roads leading in and out of the capital.

"We are *so* going to overthrow this kingdom," I said.

"I don't know, Rune. There are a lot of soldiers around. This might be harder than you think."

"C'mon, Jez. Our luck is improving. The crystal ball is working for us. And we've got our henchman and our baby, don't we?"

We glanced at Cappy, who was happily tickling our stolen baby.

"What about the princess? Why don't you see if the crystal can show us where to find one?"

"Good idea."

I ran my hand across the crystal's surface once more, but it remained dark. For ten minutes I shook it and squeezed it until finally giving up.

"What were you saying about our luck improving?" Jez asked.

"I don't need it to tell me anyway," I said. "Princesses are always in castles."

"Right," Jez said. "And when they don't just let you in the front door, they always have mile-long blond hair, which they toss out the window for you to climb.

Have you given any *serious* thought as to how you'll kidnap a princess?"

"Well," I said, rubbing my chin thoughtfully, "first I'll feed her a poison apple, then I'll stab her with a spinning wheel spindle, and if those don't work I'll bop her over the head with a glass slipper."

This earned me another eye roll from Jez.

As the afternoon faded, we traveled on, darting between groves of trees, always keeping in sight of the road but out of sight of would-be travelers. Several times we saw soldiers marching or riding horseback. I worried the baby's constant crying would give us away, but Cappy always seemed to know what the baby needed. Not only could he rock it and feed it, he also changed its diaper—swapping it out with a piece of cloth torn from one of our blankets. Then, whenever we came upon a stream or pond, he would wash out the old diaper and dry it, ready to swap it out again.

"Some evil henchman I found," I said, frowning at Cappy as he washed another diaper in the pond where we had stopped to eat. Nearby, the goat munched contentedly at a patch of grass.

"He's not so bad," Jez said. "Besides, you said yourself a good henchman should possess a quality that the villain lacked."

"Oh, and what's that? Pure stupidity?" I asked.

"How about parental instincts, Rune? Look at him! He's a natural nursemaid."

At that moment, Cappy had filled one of our spare waterskins with goat's milk and was feeding the baby while crooning a lullaby that sounded something like, "Rocky-bye baby in Cappy's arms. Cappy loves baby, la, la, la, la." He wasn't too good with the rhyming.

Cappy stood up to refill the waterskin, when he tripped over a rock and went sprawling face-first toward the ground. Amazingly, he managed to both hold on to the baby as he fell and save it from being squished under his stony body. The waterskin, however, wasn't so lucky.

"Ouch," Cappy said. Only it sounded like *oumnch* because his face was buried in the grass. He slowly raised his body to reveal the poor, tattered waterskin.

"Oh, no!" Cappy said, picking up the remains of the baby's makeshift bottle and holding it out for all to see. Then he started to cry. It was the *flutterby* all over again.

I tried to tell him not to worry. We had another waterskin and could use it if we had to—although the idea of sharing drool with Cappy and a baby was beyond gross to me. My tongue felt fuzzy just thinking about it.

Cappy continued to cry despite my reassurances. Then something remarkable happened. The waterskin rose up from Cappy's hands into the air, floating just above the baby's head. The baby stretched out its pudgy fingers toward the makeshift bottle, but it just continued to float.

"What's happening?" Jez asked.

Cappy even stopped crying, mesmerized by the floating bottle. Then the gaping tear in the waterskin began to mend. It was like watching a zipper zip itself up. In a matter of moments, the skin was repaired, good as new, and floated back into Cappy's hands.

"Okay, who did that?" I asked, looking accusingly at Jezebel.

"It wasn't me!" she said.

"Cappy?" I asked in wonder.

"Cappy no do magic," he answered. He was already refilling the waterskin with milk from the goat.

"Goat?" I asked. Hey, I'd seen animals do stranger things. The goat only bleated and continued to munch its patch of grass.

Then the baby giggled, actually *giggled at me*. It blinked and wiggled its little hands, grabbing one of its feet and sucking on its toes with a big grin on its chubby pink face.

"No way," I said.

"The baby?" Jez asked. "Maybe she's magical. She could be a witch halfsie or something."

"The Zâne did say it was special," I said, staring at the baby with keen interest. A magical baby could come in very handy . . . if only we could figure out how to control its magic.

"You, baby," I said. "Make that goat fly." I didn't have a particular interest in flying goats; really I just wanted to see another demonstration of the baby's power. Nothing happened.

"Maybe it comes and goes," Jez said with a shrug.

We spent the early evening walking parallel to the road. Cappy continued to care for the baby, and I had to grudgingly admit it was a good thing he was there. Especially since neither Jez nor I knew anything about babies. It'd been a long time since evil nursery school.

There was no more magic from the baby while we traveled. It slept. It cried. It pooped. It didn't seem all that special to me. I was beginning to wonder if the magic had really come from the goat after all.

As the evening wore on, the last of the rain clouds floated away, and the stars and moon were shining overhead. I could see the lights of a city in the distance. I knew from studying the map that it would be the capital city of the kingdom of Kaloya. It was there we'd find our princess and plot to overthrow the kingdom. Cresting a hill, we caught sight of the city gates. I knew it wouldn't be long before they were closed. We picked up our pace.

"Okay," I said. "The plan is to go in there, find the

palace, kidnap the nearest princess, and get out again without being discovered."

"Uh, Rune? How exactly are we going to do that?" Jez asked.

"No idea."

"And what about Cappy and the baby and ... uh ... the goat? We can't take them into the city," Jez said.

Cappy was crooning to the sleeping infant. He hadn't set it down since the night before when he'd first picked it up ... except for diaper changes.

"Good point," I said. "We need to stash them somewhere until we get back."

Jezebel, Cappy, and I scouted around the outskirts of the city until we found an abandoned barn. It had been partially destroyed by a fire, but half of it was still standing. Plus there was hay and a stream nearby, so Cappy and the baby could sleep and drink ... and wash out diaper poop.

"Cappy no want Runey to go," Cappy said, pouting again.

"Look here, Cappy. We ... uh ... need you to watch out for the baby while we're gone, okay? You're in charge."

"In charge?" Cappy asked. At first he looked confused, then a slow smile spread across his gargoyle face. "Cappy the boss!" he said.

"Sure, Cappy. Just stay out of sight and take care of the baby. If we don't come back in a few days, take the baby back to the forest and find the Zâne . . . the pretty flying girlies, remember? They'll help you."

Cappy nodded frantically. His tongue lolled like Wolf Junior's and it reminded me of something. Cappy's barn had a clear view of the moonlit road and the city gates.

"One more thing, Cappy. Watch the gates," I said, pointing to be sure he understood. "If you see a wolf, a *doggy*, bring him back here to the barn and tell him Rune and Jezebel are Plotting inside. He'll be dressed like a person, Cappy—dressed like us, okay?" I thought I should clarify. I didn't want to come back to a barn full of German shepherds and poodles. "Can you do that, Cappy?"

"Doggy!" he said. I had to assume that meant *yes*.

Jez and I left Cappy with some dried meat and made our way to the city gates just as they were about to close for the night. We did not see the other three figures who climbed stealthily over the city wall and followed close behind us.

CHAPTER NINE

The Plot Thickens

The capital city of Kaloya was called Dimineata, which—according to Mistress Smartyfangs—means *morning*. However, morning was far off as we made our way through the bustling city streets. Everywhere, townspeople of every kind—lords and ladies, peasants, fishermen, children—were running about finishing up the night's business and hurrying to their homes or inns for late suppers.

The first order of business was finding something to wear. Our head-to-toe black clothes weren't exactly screaming *villains!* But they didn't really say *townsfolk* either. We found some wash hanging in a random back-yard. Soon, I was dressed in a puffy white shirt with a green vest. I even managed to snatch a man's pointy, feathered hat.

I handed Jez the dress and bonnet I'd found for her.

"What is *this*?" she asked, holding the clothes away from her like it was one of the baby's soiled diapers.

"Don't get all snobby on me. You need to blend in."

"Oh, right. You really blend now, Rune. Tell me, Robin Hood"—she flicked my feathered cap—"where are Little John and your merry men?"

"Just put it on."

I tried not to laugh when she tied the bonnet over her dark hair, but I couldn't help it. She tore it off and threw it to the ground.

"Aw, Jez. Don't be like that. You just had it backward. Here."

I picked up the bonnet, pulled it onto her head, and tied it under her chin.

"There. Much better," I said, still stifling a snicker.

"Really?" she asked.

"No. Really you look like a deranged milkmaid, but there's no time to find anything else. C'mon."

Jez fumed, but she followed me as I made my way through town.

In the center of the city, we could see the palace rising up to tower over the smaller homes and shops that surrounded it. As we wound our way through the streets, I kept feeling like we were being watched. I turned around several times to look behind us, only to find that no one was there.

Finally, we reached the plaza in the center of the city where the many turrets and white marble of the palace beamed brightly, illuminated by hundreds of torches. Several of the windows radiated with a soft yellow glow. As we neared the palace, we found it surrounded by a wall that was nearly twenty feet high.

We stopped under an apple tree across the street from the main palace gate. Two uniformed guards armed with swords stood stiffly to either side.

Just across the plaza from us I saw a man with a beard wearing a cloak. He kept to the shadows, like me and Jez, but I could see him watching us suspiciously. I hoped he wasn't a guard in disguise. I picked an apple and munched, trying to look casual.

"That guy keeps staring at us," Jez said.

"I know. Maybe he's just curious."

"Maybe," Jez said, sounding unconvinced.

The night watchman called out the hour, bringing our attention back to the guards and the palace.

"So where do we start?" Jezebel asked.

"I don't know," I said. "Hey! You're a girl."

"Are you just figuring that out?" Jezebel asked. She seemed mad. Why is it girls are always mad at guys, and we never know why?

"I mean, you have more in common with a princess than I do. You're a countess. You understand all this nobility and royalty mumbo jumbo. Put yourself in her place. Where would *your* bedroom be?"

Jez gazed at the palace for a moment, then smiled and pointed. "In the penthouse."

I followed Jez's gaze up to the tallest tower, where I could just make out the silhouette of a girl standing at the candlelit window.

"How do we get up there?" I asked.

"I could fly up."

"And do what? Bite her?"

"I know a good sleeping spell," Jez said. "Let's knock out the guards, then I'll fly inside the castle and let you in."

It seemed a little risky. I generally preferred to work in the shadows, but we were short on time, and I couldn't come up with a better plan. Jez and I strode casually up to the guards as if we were going to ask them a question. Jez was about to cast the sleeping spell when the gates burst open.

"It's about time!" a man said as he hurried through the gateway. "I was beginning to think you weren't coming. I've been watching for you for hours!"

"Sir?" I asked. Surely he'd mistaken us for someone else.

"*Sire*, you mean," the man said.

Sire? This was the king! The white fur robes, jewels,

and crown atop his balding head confirmed it. And what was better, he seemed to think he knew us. If I played my cards right, I could have this clown dethroned by morning!

"I thought there were three of you," he said.

"Excuse me?" Jez asked.

"Three, *three!* I was told by Morgana to expect a warlock boy accompanied by *two* vampires. Where's the other vampire?"

Suddenly, everything was falling into place. Chad's Plot with the Morgana kids, my dad's mysterious meeting with him—apparently Chad was making his way here, to the city of Dimineata. His Plot had something to do with this man, who was obviously a king. That might make overthrowing the kingdom of Kaloya a little trickier than I thought. I had to think fast.

"Yes, there was another, but we left him outside the city to keep watch on the gates," I said. I smiled inwardly as I realized this wasn't even really a lie.

"Oh, well . . . come in. Come in. We have a lot to do. How's your . . . uh . . . mother?" the man asked as he turned to lead us into the palace.

I couldn't believe our luck. We'd come here expecting to break into the palace, and now we were being invited in by the king himself! This was going to be so easy.

"My mother?" Jez asked, uncertain.

"No child! Muma Padurii—*his* mother." The king pointed at me.

"But that's Chad's—"

"Uh. Fine," I said, poking Jez in the ribs with my elbow. "She's fine." I thought it best not to elaborate until we knew more about what Chad was Plotting.

"Good. Good," the king said, walking briskly ahead of us into the enormous palace. "She's been a great help to me, I can tell you that. When I'd decided to steal the throne from my brother, I never expected help from a witch! But she has become indispensable to my plans."

"Oh, right," I said.

Jez and I exchanged puzzled looks. I couldn't shake the feeling that something was going on here—something bigger than just a couple of villainous school Plots.

"Morgana said you would help establish me on the throne, but it's late, and I'm tired. We can start our planning tomorrow. Besides, most of the work is done. My brother and his queen are gone. Their child is my prisoner until we decide what's to be done with her. And my soldiers are patrolling the roads for any signs of the Resistance."

"Resistance?" Jez asked.

"Yes. Resistance. The reason you're here! To weed

out those who are still loyal to my brother and the queen? Come, child! They told me you were intelligent!"

"Right. Sorry. Long journey and all that. Very tired," Jez said. When the king turned away, she widened her eyes at me.

The king led us to a winding stairway, where he handed us off to a servant and bid us a good night.

"We shall talk more in the morning," he said before leaving us.

We followed the servant up the winding stone staircase. As we passed a window, I could see the gates where the guards were standing watch and the apple tree where Jez and I had stood. I nudged Jezebel and pointed out the window. I couldn't be sure, but it looked like we were in the same tower where we had seen the silhouette of the girl.

"Servant," Jez said, "can you tell us if anyone else sleeps in this tower?"

"Folks used to, but not much anymore," the servant answered. He was a dirty, underfed boy who looked even younger than us.

"What do you mean?" Jez asked.

"Used to be the king's and queen's chambers, miss. Now they's empty. Only the young prisoner sleeps here nowadays—at the tippy top in her cell."

"Prisoner?" I asked.

"O' course. She that was the princess before King Aurelio took the throne from his brother, the king that was."

"You're saying the princess is imprisoned in the top of this tower?" I asked.

"Just said that, didn' I? These'll be your rooms," the boy said, stopping outside two doors that faced each other from across the hall. "Ring if y' need anything. Pleasant night to you." Then the boy trudged back down the tower stairs.

"Jez," I said after the boy had gone. "This is perfect! All we have to do is climb this tower and kidnap the princess!"

"Just a minute, Rune. Something's going on here. What was all that about Chad's mother? And what about Morgana? She's obviously mixed up in all this. I smell trouble."

"Who cares?" I asked. "Once we get the princess, we can start working on overthrowing King Pompous-Butt and setting the princess and her family back on the throne. Two birds with one stone, Jez."

"I don't know . . . ," Jez said.

"Remember what Chad said to Master Dreadthorn? He said Morgana told him to help establish some girl's uncle on the throne. They must've meant the princess's uncle—King Aurelio. If we can put the princess's family back on the throne, Chad's Plot will have failed."

Jez frowned at me as if she couldn't decide what to do.

"I'll tell you what. Let's have a look in Master Dreadthorn's crystal. Maybe it can tell us what's going on," I offered.

Jez agreed, and we both went into one of the rooms, where I pulled the crystal ball from my pack. In a matter of seconds, we were gazing into the smooth orb.

"Show us Chad and his plans," I said to the crystal.

At first, the ball filled with a hazy red fog. Then the clouds slowly parted to reveal a scene. I saw Chad and the Morgana vampires who were Plotting with him. They were climbing over the wall of the city. I heard Jez gasp. Then the scene changed, and I saw Chad and the vampires standing at the palace gate, being questioned by the guards. He looked confused and angry. Then I saw King Aurelio coming out in his night robe but still wearing all the gaudy gold jewelry. The scene changed again, and what I saw next made me shiver. It was Chad and the Morgana kids climbing the tower stairs.

"Let's get out of here!" I told Jez.

I shoved the crystal back into its pouch. Jez was already at the door. She pulled it open to find Chad, Erzsebet Bathory, and Gilles DeRay waiting for us.

"I just *knew* we'd run into each other again, Rune," Chad said.

Busted.

Chad motioned with his hand, and two guards came in. One clapped me in irons, but Jezebel was quicker. She turned into a bat and tried to fly past Chad, but he'd been prepared for that. Gilles pulled out a net and caught Jezebel. He worked a spell I'd never heard before:

"Vampire bat,
no more of that.
Back to the form
that is the norm."

With a tiny *pop!* Jez transformed back into a girl.

"Hey!" she said, clearly as surprised as I was at the spell. Then they had irons around Jez's wrists too.

"Don't bother trying to transform again," Chad said. "The irons are bewitched to block magic."

"Let us go, Chad!" I said, angry at having been caught so easily.

"It's nothing personal, Rune. Just business." A slow, evil smile spread across Chad's bespectacled face, smushing his freckles together. I never thought freckles could be so malicious.

"And what have we here?" he asked, taking the velvet pouch from me. He opened it and dropped Dad's crystal ball into his hand. "Ooooh. He is going to be *so* mad at you. Still, you saved me the trouble of stealing it myself. Thanks, Rune. It won't be hard to find out where the Resistance is hiding now!"

"Where is the dog?" Erzsebet asked.

"The dog?"

At first I thought she meant Cappy. Then I realized she was talking about Wolf. He must've managed to spy on them without being caught. Maybe there was a chance he was still out there somewhere.

"Gone," Jez said, thinking fast. "We were attacked by a dragon, and that drooling coward ran off."

"Never trust a wolf!" Erzsebet said, smiling. Her gleaming fangs dripped over her bloodred lips.

"Why are you doing this?" I asked Chad. "I thought we were friends."

"Don't be naive, Rune. All those cookies, all those talks . . . they were just a way for me to use you to get closer to Master Dreadthorn."

"Why?" I asked. I thought I knew the answer, but I wanted to see how much information I could get out of Chad.

"To avenge my mother, of course."

Okay, I hadn't been expecting that. I figured Chad just wanted to prove to our dad that he could be a good villain (which is kind of an oxymoron, but you know what I mean). What did Muma Padurii have to do with it?

137

"No more talk, Chad. We have Plotting to do," Gilles said.

"Sorry, Rune. Duty calls."

Jezebel and I were shoved up the tower stairs by two burly guards with Chad, Erzsebet, and Gilles close behind. We arrived at the top, where the guards unlocked a barred door and threw us roughly into the dark room beyond. The door closed and locked behind us with a heavy finality.

"Well, this bites," I said.

"Not as much as *I'm* going to when I get out of here." Jez bared her fangs at the door where Chad and his Conspirators had already departed.

"*If* we get out of here," I said. "Let's face it, Jez, Chad has the crystal, Wolf's missing in action, and the only other help we have is a dog-headed gargoyle and a baby. And a goat," I added as an afterthought.

"There has to be some way out of this," Jez said.

"Maybe I can help," said a new voice. A candle suddenly flared to life to reveal the face of a beautiful young girl standing over us.

CHAPTER TEN

A Lock-Picking Princess

Are you the princess?" I asked the girl who was now fishing through my cloak trying to find my villain's tool kit. Her long blond braid brushed my cheek. She smelled like peaches.

"That's me," she said, pulling out the kit. She quickly located the tool I used for picking locks.

"A girl's hairpin?" she asked, holding it up to examine it. Her gray-green eyes reflected the candle's flickering flames.

"Hey! That looks kind of like *my* hairpin," Jez said, squinting in the candlelight.

"No, it's not. I . . . uh . . . got it from Chad," I lied.

"Well, why doesn't that surprise me?" Jez said.

"Now, Princess, if you can put it in my hand and Jez backs up to me so I can reach her chains, I could probably . . ."

"No need," the princess said.

With a speed and subtle skill that would've impressed even Master Dreadthorn, the princess picked the locks on our handcuffs, and we were free. Well, at least our *hands* were.

"That was amazing! How did you learn to do that?" I asked. I was very impressed by the princess . . . and her lock-picking skills weren't bad either.

"Ahem!" Jez said loudly.

"What?" I asked.

"If you're done drooling all over yourself, we should try to get out of here."

"She's right," the princess said. "My uncle Aurelio has taken my parents somewhere. I don't know if they're even alive, and—"

"Hold on!" I said. "Shouldn't we have introductions first? I'm Rune, and this is Jez."

"*Countess* Jezebel Izolde Valeska Dracula," Jez corrected.

"*Princess* Ileana Alexandra Veldina Nicolescu," said the princess.

The two girls sized each other up with icy stares. I decided to intervene before the whole room frosted over.

"Rune Toma Emilian Drexler," I said.

Yeah, I had some fancy names too. I held out my

hand, but the princess didn't shake it. Instead, she gave me a funny look. Jez muttered something under her breath that sounded suspiciously like *snob*.

"So, maybe you can show me that lock-picking move?" I said. "You're really good."

The princess smiled and replied, "It's not hard. You just have to—"

"Are you two done blabbering?" Jez interrupted. "Because if you are, I think I can get us out of here."

"What's the plan, Jez?"

"I'll fly out the window and get help."

"Fly out the window?" The princess looked confused.

"The flying part doesn't worry me," I said. "It's the help part I'm a little fuzzy on. Who exactly are you going to get to help us?"

"Well, Cappy is just outside the city, and—"

"No!" I said. "No way, Jez. You can't bring Cappy here. I mean, what help will he be?"

"You got a better idea?" she asked.

"Who's Cappy? Is he helping you rescue me? Is he part of the Resistance?" asked Princess Ileana.

Jez and I guffawed at the same time. It was obvious we had a little explaining to do.

"Cappy is our . . . *friend*, and Jez and I are students from . . . uh . . . a special school south of here." I was trying to explain things delicately. After all, this was a princess. Jez, however, decided to go with the direct approach.

"Look, honey, I'm a vampire. He's a warlock. Cappy is a capcaun. And we're not here to rescue you. We're here to kidnap you."

The princess looked abashed but quickly masked her surprise.

"You don't scare me, little countess," Princess Ileana said.

At that moment, the look on Jez's face was scaring *me* pretty thoroughly. I thought the princess must be brave (or really dense).

"Look here, Princess—"

"No, you look here, *Countess*. Although I've never seen a countess dressed like that before."

The princess looked Jez up and down and raised her eyebrows in an appraising sort of way.

"It's a disguise!" Jez yelled, ripping off her bonnet and throwing it to the floor. "You brainless, spoiled—"

"Leave her alone, Jezebel," I said.

Jez widened her eyes in disbelief—as if I'd somehow betrayed her—and bared her fangs. For a minute, I thought she was going to bite Ileana, which would've been very bad. Not only would it have wasted a fine lock picker, but it would also have meant finding

142

another princess. It's not like I had time to try a glass slipper on every ugly stepsister in town.

But Jez didn't bite. Instead, she turned into a bat and flew out the window.

"She really *is* a vampire!" Princess Ileana said. She didn't sound afraid so much as impressed.

"Great. Now what?" I asked. Outside, I heard a bell toll the hour. It was midnight.

"Now *I'll* get us rescued," said Ileana.

The princess stepped to the window, and I followed behind, shedding my feathered hat and changing back into my cloak. She held up the candle and waved her hand in front of it a few times as she stared down at the castle courtyard below. I followed her gaze. At first, I couldn't see anything. Then, unmistakably, a light flashed from the darkness below.

"It's almost time," she said. "Here, help me. Can you climb?"

Princess Ileana knelt down and pried one of the floor stones loose. From beneath it, she pulled out a length of rope. Every five feet or so, it was tied into a knot. She handed me the rope.

"Here, tie this to that beam up there."

"Where did you get this?" I asked as I located a sturdy rafter and fastened the rope around it. It looked solid, but I gave it a good tug and hung on it for a moment just to be sure. If the princess was planning what I thought she was planning, then we'd definitely want to test the rope *now* rather than *later*.

"My maid brought it to me last night," Ileana said.

"Why didn't you escape then?" I asked.

"Because the plan was to escape *tonight*. You're really not part of the Resistance, are you?" she asked.

"Well, no," I admitted.

"If Jezebel is really a vampire, then you must really be a warlock." It wasn't a question, so I didn't answer.

Princess Ileana eyed me for a minute as if sizing me up, then crossed to the window with the rope in one arm and the candle in the other. She signaled to the courtyard again, waving her hand in front of the candle. When the coast was clear, she dropped the rope out the window.

"But how are we going to escape the castle grounds? Won't the guards catch us?" I asked.

Ileana had seated herself on the windowsill, taking the rope in both hands.

"Who do you think I was signaling just now?" she asked. "Not all the guards are on my uncle's side."

Then she smiled impishly—reminding me of, well, *myself*—flung her legs over the sill, and began the dangerous descent, her pink gown fluttering in the breeze. I watched from above. The height was dizzying. One wrong move . . .

"Are you coming or not?" she asked.

"As long as we get something straight," I said, climbing over the sill.

"Oh? What's that?" asked the princess. She was already a third of the way down before I'd managed to get out of the window.

"You are *not* rescuing me. I'm kidnapping *you*."

"Whatever you say, Rune," Ileana said. It was too dark to see, but it sounded like she was smiling.

CHAPTER ELEVEN
Oh Brother

When we reached the courtyard, a man with a sword appeared from the shadows. He was hooded and cloaked and wore a chain mail shirt beneath a leather tunic. *We're caught!* I thought, but Princess Ileana ran to him, throwing her arms around his neck and planting a kiss on his bearded cheek.

"Highness, you're safe!" the man whispered as he smiled affectionately at the princess.

"Let's get out of here," she said.

When he stepped into the light, I could see the man's face clearly. I recognized him as the same man who'd been watching me and Jezebel in the plaza.

"Hey! Who are you?" I asked.

"No time, we'll explain later," he said. "Follow me."

The man led us across the courtyard toward the high

wall that surrounded the palace grounds. On top of the wall, a guard paced back and forth, looking away toward the plaza. We edged along just beneath him, keeping to the shadows, not daring to breathe until we reached one of the lesser side gates meant for servants' use.

Within the span of a few fluttering heartbeats, we'd slipped silently through the gate, out into the plaza, melting into the darkness. Just to be safe, nobody spoke until we were well away from the palace. We stopped to catch our breath in an alley behind a baker's shop. Then everyone spoke at once.

"Who are you?" I asked the man again.

"Who is this?" he asked the princess.

"Rune, this is Gunner Bowson, my father's oldest friend and most honored military commander. General Bowson, this is Rune. He's kidnapping me," the princess said with a wink.

"Kidnapping?" the general said, raising one eyebrow. Princess Ileana only nodded. "Now, look here, I saw this boy outside looking up at the tower. He had a girl with him. Where'd she go?"

"Uh . . . ," I said. I wasn't sure how much I wanted this man to know about me and Jez and our Plot. Ileana seemed to read my mind.

"She managed to escape," she answered.

147

General Bowson eyed both of us suspiciously, but we were still too exposed for a full inquiry. So, instead, he led us through the winding streets of the city of Dimineata. I thought it was a pretty clean getaway.

Finally, we reached a building. It looked no different from the surrounding buildings, which were all made of stone with thatched roofs. It might have been any peasant's house. There was one window, but the curtains had been pulled shut, so I couldn't see if anyone was inside. I briefly thought of calling the whole thing off right then and there. I didn't want to get trapped in a building with this tough-looking general, but I couldn't abandon my kidnapped princess now. I just didn't have time to find another one.

General Bowson knocked on the door in a strange sequence that I assumed must be a secret code. The general turned to look at the darkened alley behind us to make sure no one was watching. I followed his gaze. For a split second I thought I saw the flash of animal eyes, but there weren't any people—villains or otherwise—behind us.

The door to the little stone house opened, enveloping us in a flood of warm light. I followed the princess and the general inside, and the door closed behind.

A roaring fire welcomed us from the hearth, along with flickering candlelight all around. There must've been close to fifty men there, some talking, some eating or drinking at a long table. Upon seeing the princess (or maybe the general), several of the men stood at attention like soldiers.

"Her Highness Princess Ileana is safe at last!" the general announced. A crowd gathered around us. Apparently, *I* wasn't important enough to be introduced.

Cheers arose from the crowd of men but were quickly hushed. Obviously silence was the rule around here. General Bowson led the princess and me to a table, where we were offered warm apple cider and bread with butter. A few men broke away from the crowd to speak with General Bowson. They must have been the group leaders, because they all took turns reporting to the general. I seized the opportunity to talk with the princess.

"What exactly is this place?" I ventured to ask, but I whispered it so only Ileana would hear.

"It's the headquarters of the Resistance," said the princess. "After my uncle Aurelio stole the crown from my father, General Bowson was forced into hiding along with the other nobles and knights who were still loyal to my family. Since then, they've been gathering secretly, preparing to restore the throne to us."

A sneaking suspicion began to grow inside me— like maybe I was on the wrong side. I was a villain.

Shouldn't I be part of *Chad's* Plot? Helping the evil uncle defeat this Resistance? I mean, so far, my henchman was a sissy, my baby had practically been handed into my arms, and my "kidnapped" princess had rescued *me*. Now I was in a house with a bunch of guys who wanted to restore the kingdom to its rightful rulers. Not only was this behavior un-villain-ish, it was starting to sound suspiciously *heroic*.

Then I decided I didn't care how it got done. I'd wear a cape, learn to fly, and get a secret identity while saving damsels in distress and rescuing runaway baby carriages if that's what it took to complete this Plot!

"We have an army camped in the hills twenty miles west of the city," one of the men said. "We can be mobilized and ready to fight in two days."

"Excellent," said General Bowson. "Any word from Captain Chamberlain?"

"Not yet. He's due back any moment."

The general nodded, then turned to Princess Ileana. "Highness, we'll need to keep you somewhere safe until the battle is over. If all goes well, we can defeat Aurelio's army and restore your family to the throne."

"And if all doesn't go well?" asked Ileana.

"Then you must go into hiding," said Bowson. Then he addressed his leaders. "And now it's time for all of you to join the others encamped outside the city, but first let us pledge our devotion to our sovereign leader."

All of the men arose, each falling to one knee in front of Ileana. After swearing their loyalty to the princess, the men departed in groups of three and four so as not to attract attention. Slowly the house emptied until it was just me, Ileana, and the general.

"Now, young man, I think you and I are going to have a long chat," said the general, stroking his black beard menacingly.

His dark eyebrows bent as he scowled at me. His face was worn and tanned like leather, and his eyes were shrewd. I had a feeling he already knew more about me than I wanted. At that moment, I realized I should've run while I had the chance.

The general motioned for me to sit down, but we were interrupted by a series of knocks at the door.

"Ah, finally," said the general. "Captain Chamberlain must be back from his patrol."

The general opened the door, and before anyone could stop them, four palace guards rushed in, followed by Chad. In a matter of moments the guards had their swords to General Bowson's throat and Princess Ileana and me backed to a wall, also at sword point.

"Well, well," Chad said. "You've certainly disappointed me, Rune. I thought it would be much harder to capture a fellow warlock."

"Warlock?" the general said, glaring at me with mingled hate and suspicion. You know the phrase "If looks could kill"? Yep, I would've been dead.

"How did you know where we were?" I asked Chad.

"I saw it in *our father's* crystal," Chad said, holding up the crystal ball as proof. I didn't miss the way he emphasized *our father*. Apparently—like many amateur villains—Chad expected a big reaction from me, his captive. I decided to oblige.

"Oh! Gasp!" I said dramatically. "You're my *brother*?" I put the back of my hand to my forehead as if I were about to faint. "How could this possibly be true? Me? Brothers with a cookie-baking sissy?"

"You knew?" Chad asked. I could see the color rising in his cheeks. Villains like Chad always let insults get under their skin.

"Of course I knew," I said.

"How?" Chad asked.

I figured if I played this right, I could get Chad to reveal his plans to me in one long monologue. Amateur villains always reveal their plans prematurely. I crossed my arms and kept my lips shut. Chad got the message.

"It doesn't matter," he said. "Now that I know where

the army of the Resistance is camped, I'll send out King Aurelio's soldiers tomorrow to pulverize them! Then I'll successfully establish him on the throne, completing my Plot."

Bingo.

"But how do Muma Padurii and Morgana fit into this?" I asked. *Might as well keep the ball rolling.*

Chad threw back his curly blond head and laughed. It was kind of twittery and girly—not evil at all. Poor Chad. He couldn't even laugh like a villain.

"They both have their reasons for hating our father. Morgana organized a Plot to put Aurelio on the throne. That part, Master Dreadthorn knew about. However, Morgana also convinced Mother to help. In turn, Aurelio promised that as soon as the Resistance is no more, he'll attack Master Dreadthorn's precious school and destroy it once and for all."

I suddenly understood.

"Morgana wants Master Dreadthorn's school destroyed. Of course! She's always been jealous of him!" I said.

It seemed strange that Morgana would be jealous of Master Dreadthorn's pathetic underground dungeon when she had a castle on the sea. However, I've noticed that spoiled, snotty people always want what they can't have.

"What about Muma Padurii, though? What does she have against Dreadthorn?"

Chad didn't get a chance to answer because at that moment the door flew open, and two figures tumbled inside.

"Jez! Cappy!" I said.

At the same time, Chad was hit by the door and fell sprawling to the floor. The crystal ball flew from his hands and rolled right up to where I was standing. I scooped up the crystal. In front of me, General Bowson reached for his sword. In one swift, fluid movement he managed to disarm the guard closest to him.

"Get the princess, Cappy," shouted Jez.

"Pretty girly!" Cappy said. I heard Ileana scream, but in all the commotion, I hardly had time to care.

Jezebel practically ripped my arm off as she hauled me out the door. The other guards had been disarmed by the general. Now he covered our backs with his sword as we made our escape.

In a matter of seconds, we were fleeing through the streets. Jez *popped* into a bat; she flew ahead, ready to warn us if she saw any guards approaching. Cappy had actually scooped up Ileana and was carrying her as if she were a small child. In turn, the princess pounded at his head with her fists and demanded to be put down. Cappy didn't seem to notice.

Beside us, General Bowson still held his sword at the ready in case of attack. I could see the questions in his eyes. I had a few myself, actually, but everyone seemed to sense that now was not the time.

I thought we were making our way to the main gate, but at the last minute, Jezebel veered and led us down a dark street.

"Where are we going?" I asked.

"We can't just use the main gate. It's guarded," Jezebel said.

She stopped as we reached the wall that surrounded the city. I couldn't see any way out.

"Now what?" I asked.

"Now you climb," Jez answered.

She gestured with her wing to an enormous pine tree growing next to the wall. We ducked under the outer branches, and I could see the inside was clear of needles. It was like crawling inside a giant green umbrella. Cappy hoisted Princess Ileana above his head and into the tree. She'd stopped hitting him a few blocks back, finally realizing that he was rescuing her. Cappy followed up after her, then General Bowson.

I was still holding the crystal ball. Quickly I put it in my pack and began to climb up after the others. I could hear commotion and shouting in the city behind us. Chad must've sounded the alarm.

We reached the highest branches and made our way to the top of the wall, where Jez was already waiting for us. She was hanging upside down in true bat fashion. *Show-off.*

"Well, we made it up the wall; now how do we get down?" I asked.

"Jump," Jez answered, dropping from her branch and fluttering above the wall.

"It's got to be twenty feet high! There's no way . . ." But then I saw what she meant.

On the other side of the wall was a wagon filled with hay. It was still about a fifteen-foot drop, but the hay would break our fall. Cappy jumped first. He held out his arms and flailed them wildly as if trying to fly, landing in the hay with a *poof!* In a few moments, we had all jumped safely down and were following Jez once more toward the barn where I'd left Cappy earlier. Suddenly, I realized something was missing.

"Cappy, where's the baby?" I asked in alarm.

"She's safe," Jez answered for him. I didn't know much about babies, but I couldn't imagine it was safe to leave one alone in a barn with only a goat for company.

"You have a baby?" Ileana asked, raising an eyebrow at me.

"I'll explain later," I said.

CHAPTER TWELVE

Wolf's Tale

You did leave it alone!" I accused both Jez and Cappy when we arrived at the barn. "Great, now where am I going to get another baby?"

There was hay piled around an empty blanket. The goat was tied to an old rotted board in the corner, but the baby was nowhere in sight.

"Does this belong to you?" a voice asked from overhead. We all looked up to see the baby sitting on a rafter. And beside it, dangling upside down in midair, was—

"Wolf! You're back! Wait a second," I said to Jez. "You knew Wolf was back? Why didn't you just bring him instead of Cappy?"

I looked to see if Cappy was hurt by this, but he seemed oblivious as ever.

"Because I didn't know if we'd have to deal with

Gilles and Erzsebet," she said. "Cappy's immune to vampires. Wolf isn't."

The look on Jez's face seemed to say *Duh.*

At the sight of Cappy, the baby clapped her hands together and giggled. The magic that had been holding Wolf up dissolved, and he plummeted twenty feet straight down, landing in the soft hay.

"If I'd known what babysitting involved, I would've charged more," Wolf said.

The baby floated down from the rafters and straight into Cappy's arms.

"Well, I guess we know for sure it's magical," I said.

In a matter of seconds, General Bowson had drawn his sword, pulling Ileana behind him with his free hand.

"Look, I don't know who . . . or *what* . . . you lot are, and I'm grateful for you saving us from Aurelio's guards, but I'm taking Princess Ileana somewhere safe."

"No," Ileana said, stepping out from behind General Bowson.

"Princess?" he asked, uncertain. It was obvious the general didn't want to be in a barn with a bunch of villains, but on the other hand, he was bound to follow the princess's orders.

"General, it's obvious my uncle's plans run deeper

than we even realized. We're not the only ones affected by them. Rune's friends have saved us; we owe them a debt. That tradition is very old."

I decided not to remind Ileana that she'd already saved me from the tower, so we were technically square.

"But who exactly is Rune, I want to know! What sort of person travels with vampires and werewolves—"

"I'm not a werewolf!" said Wolf Junior, standing up and dusting off his fur.

"—and capcauns!" finished the general. "They're evil, vicious creatures!" At that moment, Cappy was rocking the baby and singing his lullaby.

"You were saying?" I asked. The general was speechless.

"I think we all have a lot to talk about," said Ileana. She sat down cross-legged on the hay, patting the space beside her as she urged the general to sit down. Finally, he relented.

"Now, where to begin?" she asked.

"Let's start with you, Wolf! I'm so glad you're not dead!" There was an awkward moment where I was sure a hug was inevitable, but we settled for patting each other on the back.

"When I got back," Jez said, "Cappy had him in a choke hold."

"He kept saying 'Runey's doggy!' over and over,"

Wolf said, grimacing as he relived the moment. "But I'm kind of exhausted. Can someone else start?"

It took us the rest of the night to finish everyone's stories. General Bowson told us all about the Resistance and how he'd secretly raised an army devoted to fighting the princess's uncle Aurelio. Ileana told us the story of how a witch had come to the palace over a month ago and cast spells on her mother and father, taking them away in the night. Uncle Aurelio had taken Ileana up to the tower, where she'd been imprisoned ever since. Then he'd claimed the crown for himself.

Jezebel and I took turns telling Wolf and the others about our misadventures with Tibix the sprite chief, and how we'd rescued Cappy. We also told them how the beautiful Zâne ladies had rescued us and charged us with "caring" for an abandoned baby. I decided to downplay the part about us being evil villains.

Finally, it was Wolf's turn. His was the story I was most anxious to hear.

"So what happened after you left us on the road?" I asked him.

"I followed Chad, Erzsebet, and Gilles through the woods. It took nearly a day before we arrived at Muma Padurii's cottage. I found a spot underneath an open window where I could eavesdrop."

Wolf explained that Muma Padurii talked to Chad

and his Conspirators about King Aurelio and her deal to help him.

"Then she took them into her cellar to show them something. Shortly afterward, Chad and the Morgana kids left."

"Tell me you didn't follow them," I said, my excitement growing.

"I didn't follow them," Wolf said, smiling. "I decided whatever Muma Padurii had in her cellar was probably worth knowing, so I waited until she left."

Wolf told us how he'd waited the rest of the day for his chance. Finally, just after dusk, Muma Padurii had gone out to look for herbs in the forest. When he was sure she had gone, Wolf crept into the house and found the door to the cellar under a braided rug. He climbed down the steps to investigate.

"It wasn't dark like I'd expected. Someone had left a candle burning. When I reached the bottom of the stairs I found a man and a woman. They were tied up."

"My parents!" said Ileana.

"Then what, Wolf?" Jez asked impatiently. She still wasn't a fan of the princess.

"The woman saw me and seemed afraid. I tried to calm her down. I took off her gag, and she told me she was a queen, that the witch had kidnapped her and her husband and was tormenting them."

Both Ileana and General Bowson winced.

"I'll have that witch's head!" The general pounded his fist into the hay.

"Did you untie Father?" Ileana asked.

Wolf hesitated. I could tell there was more, but he was reluctant to say.

"Well," he began, "the king didn't seem to need to be untied. He wasn't even gagged. His eyes were open, but he wasn't really awake. The queen said that he had been put under a spell by the witch. I didn't have time to find out more. The woman pleaded with me to free her, but . . ."

Wolf looked at me for help, but it was Ileana who spoke.

"But you couldn't, or else the witch would know someone was there," she said. She looked stricken.

"You left Her Majesty Queen Catalina and His Highness King Vasile Nicolescu tied up in a witch's cellar!" said General Bowson. His dark bushy eyebrows plummeted down over his enraged eyes. He lunged at Wolf, both hands held out like claws, ready to strangle.

I decided it was time to live up to my reputation as the son of a prominent warlock—even if I *was* only a halfsie. I worked a spell:

"Out of the pan,
into the fire . . . uh,

162

shield the wolf.
Our need is dire!"

I was trying to protect Wolf, but I ended up setting the general's pants on fire instead. My Spelling was a little rusty, okay? Anyway, it worked. The general momentarily forgot his rage in a frantic effort to put out his pants.

"Look," I said as the smoke cleared, "I think I have a plan that will help us all if you'll stop trying to skin my friend long enough to listen."

The general was obviously a little reluctant to listen to someone who had set his pants on fire, but Ileana convinced him.

"We want to overthrow King Aurelio and put your parents back on the throne," I said to Ileana.

"Why do you even care?" asked General Bowson. "What's your stake in this?"

"A witch named Morgana has enlisted Chad and his Conspirators to help establish Aurelio on the throne," I said. "Once the Resistance is defeated, Aurelio has promised Morgana that he'll attack my dad's school. I can't let that happen."

Again, I didn't bother mentioning our Plot. Call it a hunch, but I was pretty sure the general wouldn't approve of kidnapping, baby theft, and evil henchmen.

"I see," he said. "What do you propose?"

"Wolf will show me and Jez the way to Muma Padurii's house. We'll rescue Ileana's mom and dad. In the meantime, you gather your army and attack Aurelio's guards. If we coordinate this, you could have Aurelio captured by the time we return with the king and queen."

And I could complete my Plot in the nick of time, I thought, but I didn't say it out loud. It hadn't escaped my attention that I only had four days left, and it would take an entire day to get to Muma Padurii's house and another to get back to Dimineata.

"What do I do?" Ileana asked.

"You should probably stay here with Cappy," I said. I didn't want to lose track of my henchman, my stolen baby, and my "kidnapped" princess. Better to keep them all together.

"No way!" she said. "I want to go too!"

This time, the general was on my side. "It's too dangerous. Rune is right. You should remain here, Highness."

"If things go sour, Cappy can lead you to the Zâne," I added.

"Pretty flying girlies," he said, still rocking the baby in his arms.

Ileana wasn't happy with the idea of staying behind, but she finally let the matter drop.

"I have to go at once," said General Bowson. "I'll

need to warn the Resistance army that their camp is no longer secret. If that Chad kid leads Aurelio's guards straight to the camp, we might be able to circle around and attack their flank."

I had no idea what the general was talking about; warfare wasn't really my thing. However, I smiled and nodded in all the right places. Then General Bowson hugged the princess, threw a warning glance at me, and left.

Just then, Cappy had finished feeding the baby. He patted its back until it bellowed a burp that would've blown the roof off the barn if it wasn't already half-burned.

"Can I hold her?" Ileana asked Cappy, reaching out her arms for the baby.

"No!" Jez said. "She doesn't like strangers."

Cappy actually looked at me for approval (as if I cared). I nodded—earning a scowl from Jez, who stormed off to the other side of the barn. Ileana took the baby carefully in her arms.

It was almost dawn. The birds had begun their morning twittering. One of them flew down from the remaining rafters and landed on Ileana's shoulder. It was a dove. It cooed to her, and she cooed back, reminding me of all those fairy tales where little birds help storybook princesses get dressed. I wanted to gag.

"Well, aren't you pretty?" Ileana said to the baby.

"Yes, you are! Yes, you are! You're a pretty little cricket."

"Would you stop? I think I'm getting a cavity," I said. Ileana just glared at me.

"What on earth were the Zâne thinking, giving *you* a baby?" Ileana asked.

"They didn't give it to me," I said. "I stole it."

"If you say so," she said. "Is Cricket ticklish? Is she?" Ileana ran her fingers over the baby's stomach and toes. The baby giggled.

"You've given it a pet name already?" I asked.

"Pet name?" Ileana asked. She was way too absorbed in the baby. She didn't even look at me. What is it with girls and babies?

"Cricket?" I said. "Why do you keep calling it Cricket?"

"I call *her* Cricket because that's her name."

"Why do *you* get to name her?" Jezebel piped up. I could tell she was still threatened by the princess.

"I didn't name her, silly. That's just her name."

Jez looked incensed. I thought I'd better intervene before they started throwing middle names all over the place again.

"How do you know that's its name?" I asked.

"*Her* name, Rune. *Her* name!" said the princess.

"Fine. *Her* name," I said.

"A little birdie told me," Ileana answered.

"Funny."

"No, seriously. A bird told me. I can talk to most flying animals."

"Really?"

I knew several villains who could talk to animals or read animal thoughts. In fact, the Dread Master himself could communicate with his cat-a-bat, Tabs. That's why he always sent her to spy on people.

"How long have you been able to do that?" I asked. It seemed strange that an ordinary human would have such a power.

"Who cares, Rune!" Jezebel said. "It's just one birdbrain talking to another."

The princess glared at Jez.

It was around that time I decided we could all use a little sleep. We'd been up all night and had a big day ahead. Cappy took the baby from Ileana. In a few minutes, he'd laid the baby gently on a blanket and was snoring peacefully next to it.

Wolf curled up in a corner, wrapping his tail around himself and yawning, his pink tongue curling between his sharp teeth. Ileana found another spot in the hay. I lent her my blanket, which annoyed Jez so much she opted to sleep as a bat, retreating to a nice, cozy rafter in the darkest part of the barn.

We decided someone should keep watch in case Chad had people out looking for us, so I took the first shift. I curled up in my cloak on the hay just as the sun crested the horizon and watched the morning of the fourth day of my Plot slip away from me. I kept an eye on the gate and the road. Once, I saw the city gates open and a troop of Aurelio's soldiers marching out. They turned west. I hoped General Bowson was ready.

Finally, around midmorning, I awoke Wolf to take over the watch so I could get some sleep. Then, at about two in the afternoon, Wolf shook me awake. I could see the others were still sleeping.

"What is it?" I asked, groggy.

"Listen."

Wolf's ears were cocked up and he held out one of his front paws like a hunting dog pointing. He was looking west. At first I couldn't hear anything, but then, far away, I could just make out the sound of armor and swords clinking and men shouting.

"Nap time's over," I said. "We need to get Ileana's parents and get back here as quick as we can."

I whispered Jez's name up into the rafters, but she wasn't waking up. Finally, I found a rock and tossed it up at her. I missed, but it scared a couple pigeons. They fluttered around, knocking Jez off her rafter. She woke up midfall, transformed into a girl halfway to the

168

ground, and landed on her rear end in the hay with a muffled *thump*.

"Stupid pigeons!" she hissed. I didn't bother mentioning the rock I'd thrown. She didn't really need to know.

Ileana, Cappy, and baby Cricket were still asleep. I left them a quick note on parchment, a little food from Jez's pack, and the goat. I felt kind of bad leaving Ileana there with only Cappy for company. I mean, I was only concerned with protecting my investment. It's not as though I *liked* her or anything.

In the end, amid protests from Wolf and Jezebel, I decided to leave my dad's crystal ball behind too. If they had to be trapped in a barn, at least Ileana and Cappy could know what was happening. And if anything went wrong, they'd have a way to locate the Zâne.

"You're going soft, Drexler," Wolf said.

"Shut it," I answered.

We gathered our packs and checked our supplies. Then we were off to face Muma Padurii.

CHAPTER THIRTEEN
Ginger-Dread

This time, we were even stealthier than before, staying well away from the main road in case Chad had guards out looking for us. We made better time since there were no stops for diaper changes and feedings. By the time darkness had settled, we were standing just on the edge of the Forgotten Forest.

After Jez's bat-popping episodes and Wolf's seeming disappearance in the woods, I'd had my doubts about choosing them as my Conspirators, but as we navigated the murky gloom of the forest, I was thankful. Wolf's nose was like gold. He followed the scent of his own trail straight back to Muma Padurii's gingerbread house. We didn't have to worry about running into another dragon or any other creatures, because Jez flew ahead as our lookout. She was in a much better mood after leaving Princess Ileana back at the barn.

It was after midnight when we came to a clearing. In the middle, illuminated by the moonlight, was Muma Padurii's house. It was like any gingerbread cottage you might see at Christmas—only life-size. The door and windows were trimmed in frosting. It looked good enough to eat, and I found myself wanting to do just that. We all inhaled appreciatively.

"Mmm . . . smells so *good*," Jez said, taking an involuntary step forward.

"Like cookies," I said, following her into the clearing. Part of my mind screamed at me to come to my senses and get out of the moonlight. I knew I was way too exposed, but another part of me was entranced by that scent.

"It's a spell," Wolf said, pulling us back into the shadows as a shrunken, hunched figure emerged from the front door of the little cottage. We regained our wits just in time to duck down behind a boulder.

Muma Padurii muttered to herself as she shuffled along in her tattered black dress, a basket in hand. I could hardly believe that *this* woman had birthed a blond, blue-eyed, curly-haired Chad. Her silvery hair hung like spiderwebs down her mountainous humpback. She was so bent and twisted that her long, warty nose practically touched the ground.

"She's probably going to gather herbs again," Wolf

Junior said. "She went out after dusk last time. She must like to work in the dark."

"Can you blame her?" Jez asked. "I mean, she's not exactly going to win any beauty pageants. Rune, can you believe your dad and her actually—"

"Can we not talk about it?" I said as the old woman disappeared into the forest. "Okay, now's our chance. Jez, you keep lookout. Wolf and I will go in and free Ileana's parents. If all goes well, we'll be out of here long before she returns."

I should've known better. Stories are full of people showing up at the wrong moment and spoiling villainous plans. Remember Wolf's dad? The Big Bad Wolf? The hunter came in with his ax just as Wolf Senior had Red right where he wanted her. And what about the Three Bears? Caught Goldilocks asleep in their kid's bed. (Most people think Goldilocks wasn't a villain. But don't let the dimpled cheeks and blond curls fool you. Breaking and entering? Property damage? Grand theft porridge? She was evil!)

Jez flew up to the roof to keep lookout while Wolf and I made our way inside. The smell was still enticing, but it didn't work so well once we were actually *inside* Muma Padurii's gingerbread house. I could see where she'd patched cracks in the wall here and there with icing, and clumps of furry mold sprouted from the ceiling like tufts of hair from a shedding dog. Moldy gingerbread. Gross.

Other than that, the house could've belonged to any little old grandma. There was a kitchen with a fireplace burning low, where something simmered in a cauldron. The living room was dark, but I could see a sofa with a doily on the back and a rocking chair with a mangy old cat curled up asleep.

"Which way?" I asked.

"Down here," Wolf said.

I followed him down a hallway, wood floors creaking as we walked. At the end of the hall was a spare room with a braided rug. Wolf yanked it aside to reveal the cellar door. Even before he opened it, I could see the rectangular outline glowing with candlelight. I followed him down one step at a time.

"Watch out," he said.

"What? Aww, gross!" I said as I walked face-first into an old cobweb.

At the bottom of the stairs was a little square room with a dirt floor. Shelves lined the walls, each holding jars of various old-lady things like canned peaches and beets, but also less savory items such as floating eyeballs and pickled animals.

"It's like the old-lady version of my dad's study," I

said. Then I caught sight of two figures sitting in the middle of the room.

The man was thin and lanky, but well dressed with dark hair and a beard. He was loosely tied and wore the blank, smiling expression of someone who's daydreaming. The woman, on the other hand, had been gagged and was currently asleep. I could see that she looked almost exactly like Ileana. Same honey-colored hair. Same peaches-and-cream skin.

"You get the king. I'll wake her up," I said to Wolf.

I shook the woman gently. Her eyes flew open and she struggled and moaned, trying to speak.

"Hold on," I told her. I reached around and untied her gag.

"Who are you?" she whispered. Then she saw Wolf Junior. "You! You were here before," she said.

"We're here to rescue you," I said.

What? Did I just say that? I was used to lines like "Your humiliation is far from over!" or "You will soon pledge your allegiance to me!" or even "I'm going to enjoy watching you die!" (I usually said that last line to one of Chad's cookies as I held it over a glass of milk.) But I had never before said "We're here to rescue you."

This, though, was not the time to dwell on it. We had to get out of here. I untied the queen from the chair, and she gave me a quick kiss on the cheek.

"My little hero," she said.

Hero? Oh man, did I need to work on my villainous image! I wiped my cheek in revulsion.

Even though I'd managed to free her from the chair, the queen's hands had been shackled behind her back with irons like the kind Chad had used on me and Jezebel to keep us from using magic. I reached for my villain's tool kit to pick the lock, but Wolf interrupted.

"You can unlock it later," Wolf said. "We have to hurry."

I helped the queen up. Suddenly, she seemed to be scrutinizing me very closely.

"What's your name?" she asked. Her voice was a little shaky.

"I'm Rune, and this is Wolf Junior," I said.

"Rune?" she asked. Then I remembered the way Ileana had introduced herself to me and Jez. I thought maybe I was supposed to give royalty my full name.

"Rune Toma Emilian Drexler," I said. Then I didn't know what to do exactly, so I bowed (feeling like a total idiot). Wolf did the same.

"You're Rune Drexler?" There was something weird about the way the queen smiled at me, but I didn't have time to worry about it.

The king was like a zombie. We tried to coax him up the steps, but he was under a powerful spell. Finally,

Wolf just hoisted the near-comatose man over his shoulder, and we made our way back up the stairs.

I kicked the cellar door shut and threw the rug back on top of it. Then I followed Wolf down the hallway. We were almost free when—

"Rune, Wolf, run!"

"Jez?"

Her voice came from somewhere on the living room floor, but all I could see was Muma Padurii's mangy cat. It was no longer curled up in the rocking chair, but standing on the floor about three feet in front of us with something trapped under its paw. Whatever it was fluttered frantically. The cat shifted slightly, and I realized what it had caught.

"Let her go!" I yelled at the cat. "Jez, change back!"

She trembled helplessly. "I can't! I think it has something to do with his collar," she squeaked.

I noticed a metal amulet dangling from the leather band around the cat's neck. It looked like the same magical metal as the handcuffs the queen wore.

I pulled my foot back, ready to kick the mangy beast in the face.

"I wouldn't do that if I were you," a voice cackled. From the shadows, the stooped figure of Muma Padurii emerged. "I'm rather fond of Tattles. If it wasn't for him, I might not have known you were here, villain."

Cat-a-bats! Could this get any worse?

"How do you know who I am?" I asked.

"Oh, Chad's told me all about you, Rune Drexler. And your father and I go *way* back," she said, cackling madly.

"That's enough, Padurii." I was surprised to hear the queen speaking. Her sea-gray eyes had hardened to steel. "Let us go."

"I don't think so, Cat," the old woman said. I got the strange feeling that this wasn't the first time Muma Padurii and the queen had met.

"I have a score to settle with you and these brats— and your precious Veldin."

What was she talking about?

"The plan is falling neatly into place. Aurelio is king. That brat Morgana can have her way with Veldin's school. And I get what *I* want." She turned her eyes suddenly on me.

"What is it you want?" the queen asked, looking nervously from Muma Padurii to me.

"What do I want? Let's see. First, I want my youth back! Next, I want you to suffer as I have all these years! Finally, I want to be rid of Veldin's favorite boy and put *my* son in his rightful place. I want revenge!"

Muma Padurii raised her gnarled, bony fingers like cat claws. I knew a spell was coming, but I didn't have time to deflect it.

"Wing and bill
heed my will!
Peck and cluck
become a duck!"

I instinctively dropped to the floor when I heard the word *duck*. The power of the old lady's hex flew past me and hit the spellbound king full in the face. A quick puff of smoke and there was a duck standing where the king had been a moment before.

I heard the queen gasp just as the old lady reared up for another hex. She had barely opened her mouth when I came to my senses and shouted a deflecting spell:

"Cats and rats,
toads and bats,
protect me well!
Deflect the spell!"

It wasn't Pulitzer-winning material, but it worked. Nobody's pants lit on fire or anything. I could almost hear Master Stiltskin's voice congratulating me. Muma Padurii glared at me with hatred.

I decided this needed to end. Quick. I searched my mind for a spell that would work, but before I could come up with something, I felt four sharp stabs of pain in my back. Screaming in agony, I turned to see the witch's mangy cat with its claws about three feet deep into my skin! I couldn't defend myself, though, because Jez was dangling from the cat's mouth by one of her little bat feet. I twirled and grabbed at the insane beast in vain, momentarily forgetting that the witch was standing about four feet away and preparing to hex me.

Wolf stepped in to help, but the witch was ready.

"Words from dogs are overrated.
Some are better left unstated.
To avoid undue remarks,
you must speak your mind in barks."

Immediately, Wolf lost his voice. He turned to me, barking in frustration.

Queen Catalina, her hands still bound, began kicking at Muma Padurii, who only laughed.

The cat clawed up my back, but it couldn't keep its hold on both me and a fluttering bat. Jez broke free and I seized my chance.

I toppled to the floor in a stop-drop-and-roll motion trying to dislodge Tattles the Psycho Cat. I brought my weight down on him *hard* and heard a loud screech as he finally let go and shot under the sofa like a furry bullet, hissing and spitting and glaring at me. Wolf continued to bark in an alarmed sort of way, gesticulating wildly.

"What?" I asked, irritated.

Then I saw for myself. I was still on the floor as the bent shape of Muma Padurii loomed over me, her arms raised malevolently. Across the room, I saw Queen Catalina had been knocked to the ground. I was completely defenseless as the witch descended on me, her lips spreading across her face in a wicked grin like red ink across a page.

"No!" the queen shouted as she struggled to her feet. "Leave him alone!"

The witch cackled madly down at me. I was sure this was the end. Then suddenly, her wrinkled face changed from a look of triumph to one of utter shock. She turned around in a circle, batting hysterically at the back of her neck, all the while shrieking in pain and surprise. When the old woman turned again, I could see a tiny dark assailant clawing its way up the old lady's hump. It was Jezebel.

She dislodged herself and flapped around the witch's face. I noticed Tattles watching all this from his hiding place beneath the sofa. His tail was sticking out one end and thrashing like a whip as his yellow eyes followed Jezebel's fluttering motions. Almost too late I realized what he was about to do.

"Jez! The cat!" I shouted just as Tattles bounded from beneath the sofa and sprang into the air, claws extended, teeth bared.

Jezebel fluttered out of the way at the last second, and Tattles sank his claws into the space that Jezebel had occupied just moments before. Only now it contained Muma Padurii's face.

"Aaaaaargh! Geddoff, you mangy beast!" she screeched, seizing Tattles with one gnarled hand and flinging him once more beneath the sofa.

The distraction had been just what I needed. I got to my feet and fired off a spell of my own, this time offensively.

"Mindless mutter,
endless stutter,
instead of rhyme,
you'll pantomime!"

Muma Padurii had already recovered and was just in the middle of hexing me when she stopped suddenly and started flapping like a chicken. She looked confused before trying again:

"Time to flee,
time to fly,

time for Rune
to choke and—"

Only she couldn't finish her rhyme. The old woman held her hands to her throat and fell to the floor. It was like watching a really twisted game of charades.

The look in her eyes changed from fight to flight as she edged toward the door. Before I could stop her, she reached for the doorknob and slipped outside.

"Get her!" I shouted.

Jez transformed back into a girl, and she, Wolf, and I all ran after the old woman. We'd barely stepped through the door, when—

"Cappy!"

My henchman was standing just outside with the baby and Ileana. Before anyone could stop her, the witch grabbed the closest and most vulnerable being she could get her hands on—baby Cricket.

"Stay back!" the old woman screeched. She knew she was cornered, and now she was desperate. "Stay back or I'll choke her!"

Cappy howled in alarm. He took a step forward.

"Don't, Cappy!" I shouted. The princess grabbed his arm as if to restrain him just as the queen burst through the door.

"What's going on here? Ileana!" Queen Catalina

said, clearly alarmed that her daughter was in the company of a capcaun.

"I'm fine. Just stay back, Mother," Ileana said.

"That's right, my dearies," Muma Padurii said. "Just stay back! I might not be able to cast a spell, but I can still choke this redheaded whelp. Now, who does this little brat belong to?" Muma Padurii held baby Cricket out by the scruff of her neck like she was no more than a kitten. "Another one of yours, Catalina?"

"Do you get the feeling they know each other?" I whispered to Wolf and Jez. Neither the queen nor the witch heard me, though. Padurii's attention was focused on my stolen baby.

"What a tasty morsel you are!"

I cringed as I remembered that Muma Padurii liked to eat kids. I really hoped she didn't eat my baby. I was running out of time to find another one.

Just then Cricket seemed to realize the ugly, evil hag holding her by the collar was *not* Cappy. The baby's face screwed up into a pucker, then her mouth opened, unleashing a deafening cry. It cut through the still air like a knife.

"Quiet, you!" Muma Padurii said, poking the baby with one of her long yellow fingernails.

That was probably her undoing. Without warning, Muma Padurii was hoisted into the air by some unseen force. She screamed as she dangled upside down. Her black dress fell over her wrinkled face, revealing dirty gray bloomers beneath. Of all the trauma I endured that night, that was the vision that would haunt me most . . . Muma Padurii's granny underwear.

"Nasty," Jez said.

Wolf, being unable to speak, just stared in fascinated horror.

Padurii let go of baby Cricket, who floated safely back into Cappy's waiting arms. Everyone was gathered on the ground beneath the floating witch. Tattles the cat peered out from the house and seemed to sense he was on the losing side of things. He took one look at his dangling mistress and ran off into the forest.

"What should we do with her?" I asked, staring up at the witch hanging overhead.

"I've got an idea," said Ileana. She let out a series of hoots and whistles, and in a matter of moments owls began to materialize in the trees surrounding the clearing.

"You really can talk to birds!" I said.

Ileana smiled and winked at me. "Take her away, boys!"

The owls swooped across the clearing, wrapping their talons around Muma Padurii's dress. They latched on to her arms and legs and carried her away into the forest. We could hear her screaming for a long time. Then the sound finally faded and was lost.

"Mother!" Ileana shouted, running to the queen. Then she looked around. "Where's Father?"

"Oh dear!" Queen Catalina said. She ran back into the cottage. Everyone followed.

The king quacked and pecked at pieces of gingerbread on the floor. Ileana looked at me imploringly. "Can't one of you help him?"

Wolf barked helplessly, which pretty much answered for him.

I had never successfully transformed an animal into a human before. My Spelling wasn't nearly that advanced. Jez was pretty good and had come close . . . once or twice. None of this was very reassuring to Ileana. Then another voice spoke.

"Unlock these, dear," the queen said. She held out her hands, which were still bound in the magical chains. At first I thought she was talking to me, but Ileana stepped forward, pulling out one of her own hairpins and picking the queen's lock. Then the queen spoke again:

"A duck is not how you began.
You were meant to be a man.

No more bill, feather, wing,
return now to being king."

Jez, Wolf, and I just stared, our mouths hanging open. From the stunned look on Ileana's face, I could see this was a shock for her too. With a puff of smoke and an explosion of white feathers, the king transformed back into a man. He hiccuped, and a feather shot out of his mouth and floated lazily to the floor. He still looked pretty dazed.

"Can he walk?" I asked.

"He'll be able to walk in just a few minutes," the queen said. "Although it will be quite a while before he's completely restored to his old self."

"Then we should probably get going. General Bowson will have gotten back to the city by now . . . I hope."

"General Bowson?" the queen asked. Beside her the king made a strange noise. It might have been a burp or a quack.

"We can talk on the way," Jezebel said impatiently. She was obviously annoyed at being surrounded by people who outranked her.

Wolf barked at Queen Catalina as if to say *Hey, what about me!*

She worked another spell, and soon Wolf was back to normal. She even cast a healing spell on my back to mend the nasty cat scratches left by Tattles.

We started our journey back to the city. Along the way, the princess told us how she'd awoken to find my note. She and Cappy decided to follow us. They used Master Dreadthorn's crystal ball to find out which way we'd gone.

I wasn't sure how to ask Queen Catalina the bazillion questions I had. Luckily, I didn't have to ask. Ileana beat me to it.

"So, what happened back there? How did you . . . ?" she asked.

The queen glanced at the king, who was finally walking along nicely on his own but still seemed a little out of it. He smiled vaguely at a tree and waved like he was in a parade. The queen sighed as if she was about to admit something terrible but undeniable.

"I was born both a witch and a princess," she explained. "I've kept it secret for so long. Please don't tell your father."

Ileana nodded, looking thoughtful. I took advantage of the silence to ask a question of my own.

"So, why didn't you go to villain school?" I asked.

"I did," Catalina said. "But . . . oh, it's a long story."

I waited for Queen Catalina to tell us the story, but she didn't say anything else.

"But that means Ileana is a witch halfsie," Wolf said suddenly.

"Duh!" Jezebel answered.

Everyone looked at Ileana, then at the queen, but neither of them spoke.

We were all quiet for a while after that. The king came back to his senses, and with a little explaining, everything went back to normal—or as normal as it could be with royalty and villains keeping company. But I noticed the queen kept glancing at me when she thought I wasn't looking. It made me think there was something about her past that she wasn't telling us.

CHAPTER FOURTEEN

Freckled Face-Off

The going was a little slower this time, but we crossed into the kingdom of Kaloya and managed to reach the city of Dimineata just after dusk. I was surprised to find the gates wide open and unguarded. Inside, we could hear hundreds of voices shouting.

We made our way to the plaza surrounding the palace and could go no farther. A mob spilled out from the palace walls. Everywhere men and women were shouting and brandishing pitchforks and torches. As a villain, this scene made me a little uncomfortable. Angry mobs usually mean trouble for villains. Jez, Wolf, and I exchanged nervous looks, but we stood our ground. It was kind of garbled, but a chant had begun that sounded like "Down with Aurelio!"

I could see men working crowd control, but there were no guards on the palace walls.

"What's going on?" the queen asked.

"I don't know," I said. Then I spotted a familiar face. It was General Bowson. He saw me at the same time and nodded, pressing through the crowd toward us.

"We did it, boy!" he said. Then he seemed to notice I wasn't alone.

"Your Highness! Your Majesty!" He bowed to the king and queen.

"Gunner, my old friend," said the king, shaking Bowson's hand. "What's happened here?"

A few people around us recognized the king and queen. At the same time, they seemed to notice Wolf and Cappy. People started to back away nervously, and whispers were already circling our little group.

"Let's go inside and talk," the general said. He parted the crowd with a few gruff words and led all of us to the palace gate. Six or seven of the general's men were standing guard. They moved aside to let us in with sideways glances at Cappy and Wolf, then closed the gates behind us.

Even just inside the gate, it was much quieter. The general got us all up to speed on what had been happening while we were away. It turned out he'd reached the Resistance camp just in time to warn them about Chad and Aurelio's soldiers. The general's men managed to surprise Aurelio's and come up from behind to attack. Most of Aurelio's army ended up surrendering.

After the small victory, General Bowson wasted no time. He led the Resistance army into the city and marched on the palace. It was a rough, long battle, but in the end the people of the city joined in, angry at Aurelio not only for stealing the throne from his brother, the rightful king, but also for being a lousy ruler. He'd been raising taxes on the people since he'd taken the throne, and it seemed they were fed up.

"What did you do with Aurelio? And Chad and the others?" I asked.

"Well, now we come to it," General Bowson said, looking a little uncomfortable. "We can't reach them."

"What do you mean?" I asked.

"Those villain kids have Aurelio inside, and they've got enchantments on the door. We can't get in. I've been waiting for you to get here. Thought maybe you could help," the general said to me. I could tell he wasn't the kind of man who usually asked for help—especially from a kid who'd set his pants on fire.

I took a moment to formulate a plan. It seemed Erzsebet, Gilles, and Chad had combined their powers to enchant the door.

"Jez, you're not too bad at Spelling, do you think—?"

But she was already shaking her head. "I'm not powerful enough on my own."

Wolf and I were even worse at Spelling. I glanced at the queen, remembering how she had undone Padurii's spell on the king. But she shook her head at me, and I knew she wouldn't risk exposing herself by working a spell.

Alone, we weren't too powerful, but I thought together we might be able to break through the enchantment. It was worth a try.

"Everybody stay here," I said, but of course, nobody did. So we all marched up to the castle together. Jez, Wolf, and I stopped just in front of the massive oak double doors.

We took a moment to argue about the best spell for the job. Since the door was locked with magic, I couldn't just break out my hairpin this time.

"What about the Unhinging spell?" Wolf asked.

"No, that'll never work," I said. "The hinges are on the inside. What about Seal-Unseal?"

"That's for animal transformation," Jez said.

"It is? Oh, I'm thinking of Seal with a Kiss. Wait—no that's for envelopes."

"We want the Lock-Block spell," Jez said.

This was a simple unlocking spell we'd all learned when Master Stiltskin had accidentally magically locked himself in a coffin. After a little discussion, we decided it was the best option, practicing a couple times just to be sure we had the rhythm down.

"On three then?" I asked them. Wolf and Jez both nodded.

"One! Two! Three!" I shouted. Together, we unleashed the spell:

"Doorknobs and keys
open with ease.
But a good spell
works just as well."

The power of it blew the door to pieces with an explosion that rocked the ground like an earthquake.

"Whoa," Wolf said.

"Cool," Jez added.

"Let's go!"

I ran inside, followed closely by the others. Just to the left of the main entry was the throne room. I could see Aurelio sitting on the throne looking like a scared rabbit. He still wore loads of gaudy gold jewelry, but it looked like he hadn't trimmed his beard in a while, and his crown was askew atop his bald head.

To either side of him were the Morgana vampires,

Gilles and Erzsebet. And standing in front was Chad. When he saw the king and queen behind us his eyes—already huge from his thick glasses—bulged even wider.

"That's right, Chad," I said. "It's over. Muma Padurii is gone. The king and queen will be restored to the throne. Your Plot has failed."

"Stop them!" yelled Chad.

Erzsebet leaped out from behind Chad and lunged at me, her vampire fangs bared and dripping with lethal venom. I didn't have time to react, but luckily I didn't have to. Before I knew what was happening, Cappy—with baby Cricket still cradled in one arm—shoved me to the floor and took the full force of Erzsebet's bite himself. He howled with pain, then stuck out his bottom lip in a pout.

At the same time, I heard a sickening crack. Two shimmering white slivers tumbled from Erzsebet's mouth to the floor and skipped across the stone with a light tinkling noise. Erzsebet stood in shock, staring at her severed teeth, one pallid hand pressed to her bloodred lips. She fled the hall screaming in agony.

"Nice one, Cappy!" Wolf said.

Gilles took one look at Cappy and abandoned Chad, fleeing after Erzsebet.

"Cowards!" shouted Chad, but Gilles and Erzsebet

were already gone. Aurelio tried to scramble after them, but Chad cast a spell to hold him in place.

"Where do you think you're going?" he asked.

"It's over, child," Aurelio said. "Muma Padurii is gone, and—"

"No!" Chad screamed in his high-pitched, whiny voice.

"What a mama's boy," Jez said.

Chad's eyes darted from left to right. I could tell he was desperate. Cornered. I decided to try reasoning with him.

"Chad," I said. "It doesn't have to be like this. Maybe . . . maybe Master Dreadthorn will let you stay on at school. You might have to bump down a level. Start over as a Crook or something . . ."

"A Crook?" Chad asked. I thought I saw hope in his face.

"I'll talk to him for you. I'm sure we can work something out," I said.

"You . . . you'd do that for me?" Chad asked.

"What are brothers for?" I said. "Come on, Chad."

I held out my hand to him. Of course, I didn't really mean it. As soon as the weasel got close, I was going to kick his backside for putting me through all this.

Chad smiled. Slowly he stepped toward us. Everything was going to be okay.

Yeah *right*. Villains always double-cross.

Chad acted as though he was going to hug me, but instead he grabbed Ileana and yelled, "Don't anybody move."

Whew. That was close. Villains do *not* like hugs. However, hostage situations? I could deal with that. Although Chad picked the wrong hostage. That was *my* princess!

"Now, we're all taking a trip to the dungeons, where you will go quietly into individual cells. If you don't, you'll be sorry." He tightened his grip around Princess Ileana's neck. That was a mistake. I readied to make my move, but Ileana beat me to it.

The princess balled her right hand into a tiny fist and sunk it hard into Chad's freckled face. He staggered back, releasing Ileana and cupping his hands under his nose, where blood trickled from both nostrils.

"Nice one," I said appreciatively.

"Thanks," she said, shaking out her hand.

"This isn't over!" Chad tried to shout while at the same time pinching his nose to stem the bleeding. It came out kind of nasally and not really very threatening.

I lunged after him, but he cast a spell at the same moment:

"From every wall unleash a flood,
raining down as red as blood.

Though I leave you in defeat,
this revenge is just as sweet!"

I ducked aside just as a crimson torrent burst from the walls as if a dam had suddenly broken. Chad disappeared in a theatrical flash of light and smoke, but the walls kept gushing forth their scarlet deluge.

"It's blood!" shouted General Bowson.

Jez dipped her finger in the red flood, which was now up to everyone's knees. She tasted it. "It's not blood. It's—"

"Red frosting," I said. "Typical Chad."

* * *

In the hours that followed, General Bowson personally escorted Aurelio to the tower. The general had wanted to lock him in the deepest, darkest dungeon and throw away the key, but the king interceded on his brother's behalf.

"He was manipulated. He shouldn't have done what he did, but he's still my brother," the king said. I could almost relate.

Then the king and queen, along with Ileana and the general, went out to address the crowds. Cappy was busy changing baby Cricket's diaper. Jez, Wolf, and I found ourselves alone.

"Did . . . did we just complete our Plot?" Wolf said in a daze, almost like he couldn't believe it.

"Let's see," I said, pulling out the crumpled note containing my Plot. "Princess? Check. Baby? Check. Henchman?"

We looked over at Cappy, who was now rocking and feeding the baby.

"It still counts," I said, "so, check. Overthrow a kingdom?"

We took in the messy aftermath of our battle with Chad. Our clothes were stained red with frosting. We all exchanged looks.

"Check," we said together, smiling.

There was a lot of embarrassing behavior after that, high-fiving and such. I won't mention the hugging and crying either. Suffice to say, we were back to our villainous selves by the time the king and queen returned with Ileana and the general. They invited us to dine with them as their honored guests.

Once that was over, Wolf and Jez were given their own rooms, where they could catch up on a little sleep before we returned to school. And I stressed a *little*. I wasn't about to fail my Plot due to oversleeping (although I planned to get one or two winks myself).

The king and General Bowson went off together to discuss rounding up Aurelio's remaining guards and to organize a search party to go after Erzsebet, Gilles, and Chad. Cappy had fallen asleep on the floor with baby Cricket, and that left me alone with Ileana and the queen.

The queen smiled at me and brushed my dark hair out of my face. She put one arm around me and one around Ileana. As far as hugs go, it wasn't so bad. Not that I wanted to get in the habit of hugging or anything.

"Rune, I'd really like it if you could come visit us here again. I don't just mean sometimes. I mean soon and often. Maybe you could come and stay with us in the summer?" the queen asked.

This was a little unexpected. Villains don't usually get invited back, and it made me wonder again if I was on the right side here.

"I'll ask Master Dreadthorn about it," I said. "But I doubt he'll allow it."

"Let me handle him," the queen said. I wasn't sure she knew who she would be dealing with, but I let it slide.

"What about Ileana?"

"She'll be here too, of course," the queen said, looking confused.

"No, I mean, she *is* a halfsie . . . have you ever thought about her, uh, education much?"

I thought this was probably a dead-end conversation. There was no way a queen was going to let her only child grow up a villain, but I was surprised to hear Ileana speak.

"You mean you want me to go to school with you?" the princess asked.

"Sure," I said.

"Can I, Mother? Please?" Ileana asked.

"I think we might be able to make some arrangements."

CHAPTER FIFTEEN

Plot Twists

After an exhausting six days, I had finally completed my Plot. I was shown to a room, where I passed out and didn't wake up until dusk. By that time, all the others were awake and waiting for me. I had a quick meal, then—along with Jez and Wolf Junior—prepared to make the journey back to school.

It was decided that baby Cricket would stay with Ileana's family, with Cappy as her nursemaid. They even agreed to take in the goat as a palace pet.

"The Zâne were right," Jez said.

"What do you mean?" I asked.

"Do you remember what they told us the night we found the baby? 'This baby's fate is tied up with yours now. In time, you will see her gifts.' If it hadn't been for Cricket, we might have lost to Padurii."

"I suppose you're right," I said. "Thanks, baby." I could've sworn she winked at me, but I didn't mention it to anybody.

"Good-bye, Runey," Cappy said as we gathered in front of the palace doors.

He moved in for a hug, then checked himself.

"What's wrong?" I asked.

"Henchmen no give hugs," he said sadly.

"Oh, just this once, then," I said with a sigh. He grinned, crushing me in a hug that squeezed the wind out of my lungs. I endured a round of hand shaking from General Bowson and the king too.

Then the queen came forward with Ileana. They were dressed for traveling.

"Are you going somewhere?" I asked.

"Yes, I think we'll take the trip with you, if you don't mind."

I exchanged looks with Wolf and Jez. Wolf just shrugged as if to say it was okay with him.

Jez didn't look so thrilled to have company. She scowled at the princess, folded her arms, and tapped her toe loudly.

All our packs had been restocked with food—fresh sheep liver for Wolf, cocoa for Jez, and plenty of meat, cheese, and fruit for me.

"Surely you'll take a small guard with you?"

General Bowson asked the queen. His eyes flickered to me, Jez, and Wolf.

"We'll be quite safe, General," the queen said.

"Shall I come, dear?" asked the king.

"You have too much work to do here, darling. We won't be gone long."

The king seemed satisfied, but the general continued to protest. In the end the queen won out, and General Bowson gave us an armed escort to the city gates. A few minutes later Jez, Wolf, and I were on the road once more, along with our royal company.

As we traveled, we kept our eyes open for Chad, but we never saw him. We did, however, run into some old friends. It happened just before dawn. As we were walking along the road, suddenly three glowing figures appeared from out of the forest. It was the Zâne.

"Hello again," the white rose lady said. "I see you've had many strange adventures since we parted." She nodded at Queen Catalina and Princess Ileana, and eyed Wolf in a wise, knowing sort of way. I wondered if we were in trouble.

"Uh, yes," I said, hoping the beautiful flying ladies would let us pass.

"We cannot let you pass," the poppy lady said.

Nope. Guess not.

"There's something we need you to see," the daisy fairy said. "Follow us."

We didn't really have much of a choice. I was pretty sure in a battle with the powerful Zâne, we'd lose. So we all followed behind the floating ladies as they led us through the forest.

We were about ten minutes in when I started to get very nervous. I mean, I had a deadline! I was just about to risk trying a Quick Getaway spell on the Zâne when I heard a familiar sound. It was a sort of animal chittering followed by laughter and a loud splash.

The Zâne motioned for us to be quiet as we crept up to a familiar hillock. I peered over the edge, and I had to use all my power not to burst out laughing.

Below us, I could see Tibix, the sprites' chief, jumping and clapping. Behind him, several little sprites turned a crank. And hanging over a stream, dangling by their legs, were Gilles DeRay and Erzsebet Bathory.

"We found these vampires wandering in the forest and bound them so they couldn't transform. Then we turned them over to Tibix. Are they friends of yours?" asked the white rose lady. As she spoke, the little sprites let the crank go and Erzsebet and Gilles plummeted into the water.

I looked at the others. Wolf and Jezebel both smiled wickedly.

"Nope. Never saw them before in my life," I lied.

"In that case, we'll let Tibix have his fun," the white rose lady said. "We'll show you back to the road now."

When we reached the road, we said our final good-byes to the Zâne, who invited us to visit again soon. After that, we didn't see anything unusual, except once, near the middle of the forest. I thought I saw green eyes watching us from a tree, but they disappeared when we investigated.

"What do you think that was? Just a forest animal?" Wolf asked.

"I don't know, but it's not the first time I've seen something watching us," I said.

"Do you think it might be that old mangy cat of Muma Padurii's? It looked kind of like cat eyes," Jez said.

"I doubt it," I said, although I spent the rest of the trip through the forest looking over my shoulder.

We spent all morning walking under the canopy of trees. By sunset, we emerged from the oppressing forest and into open air. Although we were all tired, the sight of familiar territory (not to mention our looming deadline) gave us a boost of energy. Wolf and I practically ran the last stretch, dragging Queen Catalina and Ileana with us. Jez took advantage of the darkness and flew as a bat. We reached the doorway to the school early that evening.

Wasting no time, we made our way to Master Dreadthorn's office. Tabs was coming out just as we reached the door. She paused a moment to sniff at the newcomers and flew in excited circles around the queen, but otherwise ignored us. We knocked on the door, which opened by itself.

"Come in," my father's smooth voice sounded from inside.

"Maybe you should wait here a minute so I can introduce you?" I said to Queen Catalina and Princess Ileana.

The queen smiled and said, "Of course."

Wolf, Jez, and I found Master Dreadthorn sitting at his desk, pretending to barely notice us.

"Well?" he asked.

I couldn't contain myself.

"I did it! I did it all!"

"Ahem," Jez said from beside me.

"With help from my Conspirators, of course," I added.

"What proof do you bring?" he asked.

"Proof?" I asked, looking at Jez and Wolf. "But you never said we needed—"

"Let me get this straight, Rune. You thought you could just vacation in the forest for a few days, return without any proof of your Plot's success, and I'd *believe* you?"

"I . . . but . . ."

I looked to Jez and Wolf for help but found none. Wolf looked utterly terrified—his ears drooping, tail tucked—and Jezebel was staring at me like she was about to make me her next snack.

"If you have no proof, then—"

"They do have proof," Queen Catalina said, stepping inside the room with Ileana close behind.

"Cat!" Master Dreadthorn said, standing so suddenly that he knocked over the skull and its candle, setting the papers on his desk ablaze.

"Veldin. It's been too long!"

Then the queen rushed over to my dad, who had managed to put out the flames with his cloak, and hugged him.

He looked positively stunned.

"I take it you two know each other?" I asked, a little hurt that this had never come up before now.

"We all did," the queen said. "Veldin, Morgana, Muma Padurii, and me. We were all in school here together. Of course, back then it was Stiltskin's School for Wayward Villains."

"Wait. You were friends?" Jez asked, eyeing my dad and the queen suspiciously. I got the feeling Jez thought maybe they were more than *just* friends.

"Yes, well, as much as any villains can be, but we had a bit of—"

"A falling-out," Master Dreadthorn finished.

"Oh!" I said. This explained a lot—like how the queen and Chad's mom seemed to know each other, and why Morgana would be working with Muma Padurii to bring down Queen Catalina's kingdom and my dad's school.

"It doesn't really matter," Master Dreadthorn said crisply. "It was all long ago and is better forgotten."

I thought the queen looked hurt for a moment. She drew away from my dad, but she smiled again.

"Anyway, I know your Plot succeeded. You didn't need to drag an entire royal court here," the Dread Master said. His face revealed no emotion whatsoever.

"But a minute ago you said you didn't believe Rune!" Ileana finally spoke up. Master Dreadthorn looked at her in surprise, as if he just noticed her for the first time.

"May I present Princess Ileana?" the queen said.

Master Dreadthorn nodded stiffly, but he didn't take his eyes off the princess. Like all young villains, she squirmed under his cool gaze.

"How did you know the Plot succeeded?" I asked him boldly. Ileana looked relieved when Master Dreadthorn's eyes slid from her to me.

"I have my ways."

I glanced behind the Dread Master at the glass case

that usually contained his crystal ball. It wasn't there, of course. I cringed as I realized it was still in my backpack.

"What now?" Wolf asked from beside me.

"Now, Mr. Wolf, the three of you will attend a ceremony at ten o'clock in the dining hall, where the entire student body will be gathered. That is all."

Master Dreadthorn waved us away as if we were servants.

"Oh, and Cat," he said.

"Yes?"

He looked as if he wanted to say something to her, but then noticed everyone watching and changed his mind.

"Tabs will show you and the princess to the girls' dormitories, where you may stay for the night."

"I think I can remember the way," the queen said with a wink and a smile.

"Can you believe him?" I said as the door closed behind us. "He knew. He *knew* our Plot had succeeded, and he still wanted to make us squirm!"

"Don't be too hard on him, Rune," the queen said. "He's always been like that."

"Why didn't you tell me you knew my dad in school?" I asked.

"Oh. Well. I wasn't sure how much he'd said to you or how much he wanted you to know."

This seemed kind of lame, but I didn't dwell on it. After all, I had to get ready. A feeling of anticipation had come over me. In just a couple hours we'd celebrate, and the whole school would know I'd completed a Plot. I'd be a Fiend at last!

Jez and Wolf seemed to be thinking the same thing. They were both smiling.

"I can't wait!" Jez said.

"Let's get ready!" Wolf said. "Meet you in a few!"

We dashed off to our separate dorms.

Back in my room, I took out Eye of Newt. He'd almost gone out, but I managed to scrounge up some more fire ants for him. In no time, he was smoldering happily once more.

The room seemed too quiet. The remains from Chad's last batch of cookies lay stale and untouched. I wondered where Chad had gone and if I'd see him again. Where would he go now? I realized I might never know.

Finally, the hour drew near. I showered and changed clothes, then met Wolf in the hallway. He'd cleaned up, and was wearing a suit that looked totally ridiculous— especially on a dog.

We bumped into Jezebel by the Great Clock, and I almost didn't recognize her. She had traded in her traveling cloak for a black dress with a purple satin lining and a high collar. Her hair was curled and pinned up. She looked amazing.

Wolf let out a little howl and waggled his eyebrows at me, then ran ahead, leaving Jez and me alone.

"Whoa," I said, taking in her outfit.

"Do you like it?" she asked, twirling. "My dad bought it for me."

I was reminded of the way she had twirled in her lambs' leaf towel, and suddenly felt like something was stuck in my throat and my cheeks were burning. I loosened my collar, but it didn't help.

"Uh," I croaked. "You look . . . beautiful."

Jez stopped twirling and smiled at me, her violet eyes sparkling. I offered her my arm, and together we made our way to the dining cave, where we caught up with Wolf Junior.

We peeked around the doorway, catching a glimpse of the enormous cavern, which had been decorated for the occasion. Glittering candlelight reflected from the water that glided in smooth, even sheets down the glistening walls. Skulls adorned every table, no doubt donated by Jez's dad.

"This is it!" Wolf said excitedly, drooling a little on his collar. "I can't believe we did it!"

"No more kitchen duties. We're going to be Fiends!"

"Ahem," Jez said.

"Except for Countess Jezebel, of course, who will be an Apprentice," I amended.

"Finally!" said Jez. "Daddy will be so proud of me!"

I wondered what my own dad thought. He hadn't seemed very excited that I'd completed my Plot, but had I really expected anything else?

We stood outside, listening to the excited chatter of the entire student body seated within.

When we stepped through the doorway everyone stared at us, and the buzzing chatter grew louder as whispers and gossip flew around the hall. Clearly, a rumor about our Plot had already spread. At the front of the cavernous hall was Master Dreadthorn. He motioned for us to join him on the platform. Here, a table had been set up just for us, and I noticed a few other figures sitting at the table.

One was Wolf's dad, Big Bad Wolf Senior. His tongue lolled, and his tail wagged happily. To his left was Jez's dad, Count Dracula. He nodded his pale face as Jezebel approached, and she beamed up at him, unable to hide her happiness.

Sitting next to my dad were Queen Catalina and Princess Ileana. They both waved and smiled at me. I flashed back a grin, caught my dad watching me, and quickly wiped the smile off my face. Then I noticed someone else.

Sitting next to the count—to my surprise—was Morgana. She wore head-to-toe white and looked more stunning than ever. However, her painted-on smile did not reach her emerald eyes. She kept watch on me as I entered the room. I got the sinking feeling that I'd made a new enemy.

"Attention," the Dread Master said after we'd reached the platform. Even though he spoke quietly, the room grew quickly silent.

"Today, a villainous Plot has been completed. Unfortunately, it was not the Plot you were all aware of. I am afraid Chad and *Morgana's* students failed utterly in their Plot."

Nobody missed the emphasis the Dread Master put on Morgana's name. Her lips pursed, her eyes narrowed at Master Dreadthorn, and I could see her knuckles turning white as they strangled her napkin. Master Dreadthorn pretended not to notice.

"However, some of our own students took on a very dangerous, very secretive Plot, and I am pleased to report they succeeded! A baby was stolen, a princess kidnapped, a capcaun made into a villain's henchman, and a kingdom overthrown!"

The hall erupted in cheers.

"Would you like to meet the Conspirators?"

More cheers. Wolf's dad was howling. Dracula held

out one of his hands and was patting the top of it delicately with his other hand. Morgana didn't clap at all.

"Big Bad Wolf Junior, please come forward."

Wolf moved next to my dad, who placed a medal around his neck.

"You are awarded the status of Fiend!"

More cheers. Wolf left a puddle of happy-drool on the floor, and his wagging tail made contact with the count's crystal goblet, knocking the drink right into the vampire's pallid face.

I was happy to see the flying liquid hadn't missed Morgana. Her white dress was now spotted with red . . . and so was her face. A small skirmish broke out in which Morgana accused Dreadthorn of causing Wolf Junior to splash her on purpose. Dracula grabbed Wolf Junior's tale as if to bite it. Wolf Senior grabbed Dracula by the hair, exposing his neck as if to bite *him* for trying to bite Wolf Junior. And it all ended with Morgana throwing her drink at Wolf Senior, missing, and splashing her beloved Count Dracula full in the face . . . again.

After exchanging several napkins and a round of insincere apologies, the chaos finally settled down. Then it was Jez's turn.

"Countess Jezebel Dracula," my father said.

Jez joined Wolf (whose tail was now hanging limply behind him) next to Master Dreadthorn.

"You are awarded the status of Apprentice!"

The hall erupted again as Master Dreadthorn gave Jez her medal. There were even a few whistles and catcalls from some of the vampire boys. I made mental note of who they were so I could hex them later. Then dad called me up.

"Rune Drexler," he said with a long pause. He looked as if it pained him to admit my success. Finally, he got the rest of the words out. "You are awarded the status of Fiend!"

A slow smile spread across my face. No more kitchen duties. Everyone was clapping. I was finally a Fiend. I felt like nothing could ruin this moment. Then the Dread Master whispered to me, "I want to see you in my study. Midnight."

I deflated like a balloon. What could he possibly want to see me for? A familiar twitching began in my left eye.

"Congratulations to all the Conspirators!" my father said aloud. Then we feasted. Jez's dad even looked the other way as she enjoyed a well-earned cup of cocoa.

I decided to forget about my dad for a while. Maybe he just wanted to congratulate me personally. Slowly, I relaxed and enjoyed the moment. It was the best night I could ever remember having at Master Dreadthorn's School for Wayward Villains.

In honor of our accomplishments, all classes had been canceled for the rest of the night. So, after the feast, everyone enjoyed a little after-party out in the moonlight. The vampires plied Jez with questions about her role in the Plot, while Wolf gave me an if-you-can't-beat-them-join-them shrug and howled at the moon with the werewolf halfsies. Everyone was buzzing about Chad's Plot failing, and I was bombarded by Crooks and Rogues all wanting to get in line to be my new roommate. Yeah. I was popular.

"Well done, Rune," Princess Ileana said to me. "Turns out being kidnapped was one of the best things to ever happen to me."

"Thanks," I said with a laugh. "So, your mom might let you come here?" I nodded toward Queen Catalina, who was talking to Master Dreadthorn and Master Stiltskin.

"I think she's arranging it right now. I can't wait!"

I secretly hoped Queen Catalina would let Ileana enroll at Master Dreadthorn's School. It might be cool to have her around. She was, after all, a very skilled lock picker. She definitely had villain potential.

I was talking to Jez and Wolf when Queen Catalina caught up with us. She hugged each one of us in turn, first Jez, then Wolf—both of whom stood rigid and stiff, looking very uncomfortable. Last, she hugged me.

"I've arranged with your father to have you visit next summer."

"Really?" I asked in disbelief.

Master Dreadthorn was going to let me have *fun*? Who could've predicted that?

"There are a few things I still don't understand, though," I said as the queen and I stepped away from the crowd.

"Oh?" she asked.

"What exactly happened between all of you? All those years ago? I mean, whatever it was made Padurii pretty angry. And Morgana keeps giving me the evil eye, and obviously something happened between you and my dad."

"Veldin doesn't like to talk about it. We both swore never to bring it up, but with all that's happened, well . . ." She trailed off for a moment before speaking again.

"When I first came to this school, I was already a princess. My father was a king, my mother a sorceress, but my father kept it secret from the public. If word got out he'd married a villain, it would have ruined his political career. So my mother secretly enrolled me, telling my father I was attending a finishing school. I quickly made allies and found I was rather talented in Spelling and lock picking."

I smiled, thinking of Ileana's skills.

"My closest allies were Veldin, Morgana, and Muma Padurii. Veldin and Morgana were very competitive—always fighting to be best in our class. And Padurii . . ."

"Was ugly and evil?" I asked.

"No," the queen said, sounding surprised. "She was beautiful."

"What!" Muma Padurii had *really* let herself go in the last few years.

"She was lovely and *in* love. With your father."

"Oh," I said. The *L*-word was always a bit uncomfortable for villains, plus I couldn't really picture anyone being in love with the Dread Master.

"But he had already given his heart to somebody else."

"Really? Who?" I asked.

She smiled at me. "Oh!" I said. "You?"

"That's right. In fact, during our final year at school, we were secretly married."

"Whoa." I was completely stunned. I couldn't believe how little I knew about my own father.

"It didn't last, though," the queen continued. "When Padurii found out, she was heartbroken. She wrote a letter to my father, revealing that I was actually attending a school for villains. He forced me to leave Veldin and arranged for me to marry another man that same month."

"Your husband, the king?" I asked.

"That's right."

"But how did Padurii and my dad . . . ? I mean, you know, where did Chad come from?"

"Padurii tricked your father. She used a spell to take on my likeness. He thought she was me. When he found out the truth, there was a fight. She cast a spell, but it backfired, aging her into an ugly old hunchback."

"So that's why she's so . . . you know. And Chad's all blond and blue eyed?"

"Right," said Queen Catalina.

"Wow," was all I could say. "And that's why she was so mad and wanted revenge?"

"Yes," said the queen. "Actually, it's a pretty amazing coincidence, isn't it?"

"What?" I asked.

"That Veldin gave you a Plot leading you to my front doorstep. That you were able to restore my kingdom and save me and Ileana."

"Whoa, hold on a second. I see what you're getting at," I said. "But it had to be a coincidence. I mean, it's not like he *sent* me to your kingdom. I could've chosen *any* kingdom to overthrow."

But was that true? What had made us choose to go to the kingdom of Kaloya in the first place? Then I remembered Jez had overheard my dad talking about it on Cook's pirate ship the night I told him that Wolf

219

and Jez were my Conspirators. Was it possible my dad had planted that information? Staged a conversation when he knew one of my Conspirators would be listening? Then sent me not as a villain to overthrow a kingdom but to *save* the woman he used to love?

There was no way. Because if it was true, that would mean Master Dreadthorn, my evil villain father, had done something *heroic*. I just couldn't believe that. But now that the idea was there, I couldn't stop thinking about it either.

I noticed Queen Catalina was watching the emotions play across my face. She looked so much like Ileana. It made me think of something.

"Hey, did you know my mother back then?" I asked.

The queen paused a moment, pursing her lips.

"If your father hasn't mentioned her, then I don't think I should either."

I wanted to ask more, but the queen excused herself, and I was left alone.

Later, in the middle of the party, I managed to slip away. It was nearing midnight, and I had just remembered something important. I stopped by my room to pick up the Dread Master's crystal ball.

Soon, I made my way to Master Dreadthorn's study. I knocked, but no one answered, and the door was locked. Quickly I produced my stolen key and let myself inside. I was just replacing the crystal ball when the door opened and in stepped Master Dreadthorn. *Busted.*

"What do you think you're doing?" he demanded.

"Uh . . . Chad stole your crystal ball, but don't worry. I got it back for you," I lied.

"Indeed? And you broke into my study to return it. How thoughtful."

Somehow I didn't think he was being sincere.

"Sit down, Rune," the Dread Master said.

I took a seat in the leather chair while Master Dreadthorn walked around his desk to sit opposite me. Just then, Tabs jumped between us to land on the desktop. She blinked at me with her green cat-a-bat eyes, and I flashed back to the eyes I had seen during my Plot. So *that's* how Master Dreadthorn knew what happened on our Plot! He'd had Tabs trailing me the entire time!

A thought suddenly sprang to my mind, something I'd subconsciously been wondering since I started my Plot. I uttered it aloud before I knew what I was doing.

"Did you know that Chad would fail?" I asked. "Or was it me you wanted to fail?"

There was an endless, menacing pause. It might have only been the span of two or three heartbeats, but it seemed like an eternity to me.

"Am I not the master of this school, Rune?"

"Yes, uh . . . no . . . uh . . ." *Cat-a-bats!* I never could figure out how to correctly answer questions like that. It was like trying to work out a puzzle . . . something to do with double negatives . . .

"I never want any of my students to fail. It does not reflect well on a school's master when students fail."

I should've known he'd say something like that.

"Then why pit us against each other? I know you told Chad not to let me succeed. And you told me to do the same to him."

"I simply gave each of you what you needed to be successful villains. Chad was too soft for a villain. I knew he had ulterior motives thanks to Morgana and his mother, and that was encouraging. However, I thought a little jealousy might motivate him to try even harder. You, on the other hand, are a natural leader, but you get bored, Rune. I motivated *you* by making you think you had to compete with Chad."

This was the most my father had ever said to me in one sitting. I decided to keep the ball rolling.

"I know he's my brother," I said.

"What of it?"

"Well, are you ever going to talk about what happened? You know, back then?"

"The past is past. I will not speak of it," he said. That

222

was the Master Dreadthorn I knew. Cold. Uncommunicative. And kind of mean. I almost asked him about my mother, but I decided to let it go. For now.

Instead I asked, "Is he going to be exiled?"

"I don't know what will become of Chad." The Dread Master's tone alerted me that the topic of Chad was now closed. Time to change the subject.

"What will happen to Morgana?" I asked.

"Should something happen to her?" Master Dreadthorn looked confused.

"Shouldn't she be punished or anything? I mean, she tried to destroy your school!"

"Isn't that what villains do?" he asked. I couldn't really argue.

"And what about Princess Ileana? You know she's part witch," I said. He looked at me for a long time. I started to wonder if he'd heard my question.

"Ileana is a special case. It would've been easier if she had just lived a quiet life with her mother, but I suppose after all that's happened . . . well . . . I have a feeling you'll be seeing Ileana again very soon."

This cheered me up immensely. I stood to leave and had just made it to the door when Master Dreadthorn spoke.

"Oh, Rune?" he said.

"Yes?"

"You don't really believe I'm finished with you?"

I sat back down, wary.

"Don't think it's escaped my attention how miserably you performed on this Plot."

"*What?*" I shouted. "I thought I did pretty good for my first Plot."

"Don't be ridiculous, Rune. Your henchman turned out to be a nursemaid. You had to be rescued by your *kidnapped* princess. You ended up restoring a kingdom to its rightful rulers. And even that redheaded little brat was more capable than you were."

"But, but . . ." I had no argument.

"At least *Chad* was backstabbing. At least *Chad* had ulterior motives. Have I taught you nothing, Rune?"

"But, but . . ." My eye was practically convulsing. Was he seriously comparing me to sniveling, cookie-baking, freckled . . .

"And on top of it all, you broke into my study and stole my crystal!"

A very dangerous vein throbbed on the Dread Master's left temple. (It reminded me a little of my own twitching eye.) Slowly the throbbing subsided and he resumed his smooth, indifferent tone.

"At least that act showed *some* initiative. Well done on that account, I suppose."

I couldn't believe my ears. Did my dad just . . . *compliment* me? I felt a little warm and fuzzy inside.

"However, your thievery will not go unpunished."

So much for warm and fuzzy.

"Answer this riddle for me, Rune. What's green and slippery and is about to get cleaned up by a Fiend who had the audacity to steal my crystal?"

"Slug slime?" I asked in a small voice, the last vestige of my good mood flying right out the door.

"Very good, Rune," the Dread Master said. "You'll make a fine Fiend."

ACKNOWLEDGMENTS

This book really began early one morning as I woke up with an idea in my head and scrambled for a pencil and paper. I jotted down just a few words about a villain school and a boy whose father was disappointed with him. That story grew into the book you are now holding.

That might never have happened were it not for the following people: Nancy Gallt, thanks for your initial interest in my story. Marietta Zacker, you walked me through every step of this wonderful experience, and I am eternally grateful. Caroline Abbey, my editor at Bloomsbury, you made my words shine. Thanks to my family and friends for their patient listening and high expectations. Thanks to the teachers who were fun and thoughtful and tough on me. Thanks to the

Greatest Author who inspires me every day. My gratitude to everyone who had a hand in this story as it made its way from mind to page to shelf. And thank you, reader, for choosing this book.

Stephanie S. Sanders

Great villains begin with a Plot, and Stephanie S. Sanders is no exception. While she would not call herself a villain, she is the mastermind who Plots against her characters, constantly throwing them into the paths of wicked gingerbread witches, cookie-baking two-faced roommates, and perhaps the worst of all . . . evil school masters. She lives in Iowa with her two mischievous girls and her deceptively sweet husband, Benjamin. When she's not Plotting against her own characters, Stephanie is likely to be found creating strange works of art, taking incriminating photographs, reading dangerous books, or eating indecent amounts of chocolate.

www.stephsanders.com
www.villainkids.com